Copyright © 2018 by Sabrina Rose

This book is a work of fiction. Names, characters, places, and incidents either are the product of the author's imagination or are used fictitiously and are not to be construed as real. Any resemblance to actual persons, living or dead, business establishments, events, or locales or, is entirely coincidental. No portion of this book may be used or reproduced in any manner whatsoever without writer permission except in the case of brief quotations embodied in critical articles and reviews.

Sabrina's Contact Info:

Instagram: Calirosee_

Email: Calirosee1221@gmail.com

Candace

"I'm coming, I'm coming!"

I yelled into my cellphone to my best friend, Emerald. I knew she was getting impatient waiting on me but once she sees me, she'll understand why. Of course, I was going to look sexy tonight. I finally did it, opened my own salon. No matter how long it took to get there, that was the number one goal. *Candy* named after yours truly of course. But now it was time to celebrate! I grabbed my black Chanel bag and put my phone inside of it. Not before looking myself over once more in the mirror. My red dress fitted me to a T and complimented my chocolate skin tone. Well, what was left of the dress, it left a little to the imagination. The dress stopped mid-thigh with the back out right above my ass and the black pumps I had on went perfectly with it. Yeah, I was showing out tonight, I deserved it.

Rolling my eyes as I locked my front door, Emerald was beeping her horn repeatedly. Rushing to her car, I knew she was going to open her mouth to say something slick because that was just her.

"About damn time! I don't know if I should be upset or what, only because you look so good! Congrats! I'm so proud of you baby!" she yelled while reaching over to hug me. *Bipolar ass!*

But I wasn't the only one looking bomb. Emerald had on a V neck Navy Blue sequin dress that I picked out for her the day before and a pair of nude pumps. Also, stopping at her mid-thigh. I knew the dress was going to go well with her caramel skin tone and shape that she always tried to hide.

"Thanks girl," I said grinning from ear to ear. Like I said, I deserved it and was very proud of myself.

"Now tell me about the club we're going to again?" Emerald asked.

"Well, my cousin Yasmine said it's a new club opening downtown. I think it's called Nightlife or Dark. I don't know nor does it matter really," I laughed as putting the address in the GPS, turning up the AC.

"Thirty minutes away? That's not bad. I think I know exactly what building she's talking about too," she said.

Most likely she did. Emerald is a Realtor and a damn good one. She's the reason why I was so lucky to get the place that I have now. Starting the car and turning the music up, we were on our way.

Pulling up to the club, the line was long as hell. I'm glad I went with my instincts and told Yasmine to book us a section. Walking up to the club I saw BLACKOUT, in big blue neon lights. *Oh, so that's the name of the club*, I thought. After telling the bouncers my name we proceeded inside the club following a worker to our section. Looking around the club as we sat down, there wasn't that many lights. Hence the name, *Blackout*. The bars and the tables were made of thick glass with neon blue lights inside of the glass were colorful tropical fish. This shit was dope!

"Bitch! Are those real fish?!" Emerald yelled over the music pointing at the table.

"Looks like it to me," I said.

"Oh yeah, I like this club!" she laughed as the bottle girls brought us our two bottles of Patron. We loved us some tequila. Pouring two shots each we took them both back.

"We are going to be fucked up tonight," Em said with a screwed-up face from the effects of the Patron.

That's the plan, I thought.

"Congratsssssss!" I heard my cousin Yasmine screaming.

Yasmine was the tallest out of all three of us and had some nice long chocolate legs that gave her, her height. She always wore her legs out constantly making it known they was her best feature. Yes, so here she was in an all-white one-piece shorts jumper and some red stripper looking shoes. They were cute, but I don't know how she was so comfortable wearing them, no matter how much practice she had in them. She came up to me and hugged me and I thanked her.

"What took you guys so long?" She asked as I saw Emerald giving me the side eye.

Yasmine must have noticed too because she just laughed and gave Emerald a hug.

"I heard the owner of the club was here and fineeeeee as hell and paid might I add!" Yasmine said excitedly looking around.

"How fine you are talking?" I asked.

"Fine, fine. Finer than fine! Girl, I can't even compare. Shit, I don't even know how he looks but all the bottle girls I was occupying my time with waiting on y'all calling dibs," she laughed.

"Well shit let them have him. Nobody got time to be competing with no silly hoes. Here take your two shots they are waiting on you," I laughed as I passed her the two shots of Patron. She took them back like a pro. No screwed-up face or nothing.

"Now it's time to turn up!" She yelled.

"Yesss Candy! It's your birthday!" I heard Emerald drunkenly yell as I danced to Juvenile's song "Back That Ass Up". Yasmine was smacking my ass while recording me on her Snap chat. I hated when she did that because she had a big fan base from her "entertaining career". Being a stripper is what I call it but, to each its own.

Shit, it wasn't even my birthday, but it damn sure felt like it! I could never sit down when I heard this song. Then again, who could?

"Hold on y'all, I'm going to the bathroom," I told them walking away.

Wherever the damn bathroom was, I thought. As I approached the back of the club. The music was wearing out as I got closer to the elevator. I figured why not just take the elevator to another level and use that bathroom, so I don't have to wait in line? I really needed to go badly! This club was packed right now so I knew the bathroom line would be never ending. I got on the elevator and saw it was only two floors available. I pressed the second floor hoping by the grace of god I found a bathroom.

Walking off the elevator the second floor had see through windows everywhere. I saw the entire bottom level of the club. Yeah, this club was official. Taking a few steps, I finally saw the bathroom sign in silver bold letters. *Thank god,* I thought. Opening the door to the bathroom I was in awe. Just like downstairs with everything being made of glass, so was the bathroom sinks filled up with beautiful tropical fish also. *I'm definitely going to get a selfie in this bathroom.*

It felt like I was peeing for an hour. Finally, I was able to wash my hands and freshen up a little. Applying my favorite MAC lip gloss on, I took a few pictures in the mirror. I couldn't wait to show Em and Yasmine my pictures and gloat. I just knew they were going to hate. Opening the bathroom door, I heard a guy talking. Looking around I didn't see him, but I heard him ending what sounded like a phone call.

"Hold on I'm going to call you back. Something caught my eye," he told the caller.

"Devil in a red dress. You lost?" I heard him ask.

Well, I had on a red dress so I'm pretty sure he was talking to me. I started to speed walk now.

"No. Thank you for asking," I quickly replied.

I didn't even look back. I just kept walking the direction of the elevator.

Of course, the elevator was taking its time but was fast as lighting to get me up here. Looking straight forward I felt him getting closer. I knew I should've never come up here all alone. Fuck! Accepting my fate, I turned around and what I saw was not what I was imagining. Shit, am I the devil or him? I didn't know if I was supposed to be scared or infatuated with his physical features. As he got closer, I started to get an even better look at him. From a distance or close it didn't even matter. This man was fine! He was brown skinned — No scratch that he was milk chocolate and I loved me some milk chocolate. To eat it, to drink it, it didn't even matter to me. His cut looked fresh as if he just got up from the barber chair. With some long pretty eyelashes and some sexy bedroom eyes and—.

"Nasir, and you?" I saw him with his hand out, cutting my fantasizing about him short.

"Oh, umm Candy," I said as I shook his hand. I never felt any hands as smooth before.

"Umm Candy? Are you sure that's your name?" He asked me laughing.

Oh, lawd he got dimples too? I can just imagine what our babies would look like.

"Yes," I said looking back at the elevator. I was obviously in the daze by this handsome man that was about to kill me and here I am lusting over him and thinking about our future. No more tequila tonight if I get out of this alive.

"Any reason why you're up here and not down there?" Nasir asked, looking at the lower level of the club.

"I just wanted to be in and out the bathroom. That's all."

"Well don't go roaming around places you're not familiar with. Next time it probably won't be someone as nice as me you'll bump into."

"I wouldn't mind," I said.

"Huh?" he asked.

"Nothing good night," I replied.

With that being said he walked away, leaving his cologne lingering in the air.

Ding! The elevator opened as I walked on.

Shit, I think I got to pee again, I laughed to myself.

Walking off the elevator I saw Yasmine and Emerald getting into it with a group of girls. Most likely Yasmine started this because she always does every time we go out. *It's time to go.*

"All y'all bitches is just madddd!" Yasmine screamed as I grabbed her and walked towards the club entrance with Emerald walking behind us. Turning around, I saw Nasir again and he winked at me, so I waved him goodbye. I was going to sleep real good tonight. *Congratulations to me...*

Emerald

Looking out the window, I was waiting for my second client of the day to arrive to the house I had to show him. I examined the view which was beautiful of the city. The house was in Jersey City, so it was about an hour ride away from New York City. I made sure I got here with more than enough time to spare before my client arrived. The appointment was for noon and now it was ten minutes after. I heard a car door close assuming it was him and I was right. He walked through the door and his cologne hit me right in the face.

"Good afternoon Mr. Forrest thank you for coming," I greeted him as I shook his hand.

"No problem. You can just call me Trey," he smiled.

We only talked over the phone, so I never saw him in person. He was light skinned with some beautiful hazel eyes. Very tall, not real big or too small. From what I can see he had a few tattoos on his arm. I wonder what he did for a living to be paying for a nice house like this.

"Okay, so Trey are you ready to take a tour of hopefully your new home?"

I knew he was going to get this home because it was beautiful and offered a whole lot.

"Yup, lead the way Ms. Emerald."

Starting from the basement, we made our way to the living room which was very spacious. My whole apartment was probably the size of just the living room. I showed him the kitchen next, which was the best part of the house in my opinion. The marble cabinets are what took the cake. Also, with a big walk through, it was very spacious. Nodding his head in agreement Trey put his thumbs up and I got overly excited deep down knowing this commission was going to be a blessing. This would be the biggest ever that I've ever received.

"Okay so next is upstairs it has three rooms and two bathrooms. Would you like to see the two guest rooms or the master bedroom first?" I asked him.

"Whichever you prefer."

"Okay so the smaller rooms it is," I laughed.

Walking up the stairs I felt his eyes watching me. More than likely he was looking at my behind being a normal man. I knew my pencil skirt was giving him the just the view he needed. No, that wasn't my intentions but hey my body has a mind of its own.

Showing him the first one and then second one I asked, "Does it look like a good size for your family?"

"It's no family, just me," he replied.

"Oh, okay well this would be a great home to start your family in," I said obviously trying to sell the house even more.

"Don't worry I want this home. My mind is already made up."

"But you didn't even see the master bedroom yet."

"If I already made up my decision without seeing the master bedroom, I know it has to be just as nice as everything else. Also, I have a feeling you wouldn't sell me anything that's not up to par, right? Ms. Emerald." He asked me with a flirtatious look. I knew that be coming soon. Usually, the men I sold homes and apartments to tend to flirt with me. Which is all fine and dandy because I knew each would be a seller.

"Yes, Trey you're definitely right," I laughed.

Lastly, coming to the door of the master bedroom I moved out the way so he can have the honors of opening the door.

"Lead the way," I told him.

He opened the door nodding his head again. I knew he would like the room. It had a beautiful view of the city just like the living room that made this a seller.

"Sold," he laughed.

"Okay great. I'm glad that you're pleased with your new home. From what I told you earlier the process takes a little but we will follow up and get you in your new home as quickly as possible," I told him while shaking his hand and imaging the shopping spree I'm definitely going on when this deal closes.

I walked back down the stairs with him following closely behind me.

During small talk as I showed him the home, we gotten to know each other, just growing a relationship with my client. He invited me to a barbecue that I told him I would attend. One of his friends were throwing it. I knew I wasn't going.

Walking to our cars, suddenly he stopped walking and started walking in the direction I was walking...

"So, Ms. Emerald I hope to see you next week," he said.

"Yes, you will," I told him knowing that I was lying.

"Don't make me come looking for you," he said opening my car door for me.

"Thank you and nope I'll be there."

I laughed closing the door. Driving past his car, I beeped my horn and proceeded to go home. I'm filling up a few carts tonight just to be ready to complete those orders when my commission come kicking in.

One week later...

Grabbing the second bottle of Wine and pouring me a cup I put the bottle back down onto my bar.

"Bartender can I get a refillllll," Candy laughed mimicking Elle Varner.

"I'm not a damn bartender, get up and pour it yourself," I told her and sat down.

"I'll pour you a drink baby," Yasmine replied.

Her ass just wanted to pour herself another drink too.

"I'm tired of y'all Heffas coming over here drinking up all my damn wine!"

"Girl please you should be honored to be in my presence," Yasmine conceited ass responded.

"Yeah okay," I laughed.

We were just hanging out lounging watching romantic movies. We were all hopeless romantics deep down inside and this was the usual when we didn't have to work.

We just finished watching "PS I love you". One of my favorites. I always tried to get them to watch it, but they always requested something else because they never heard of the movie. As if that made any sense.

"Emerald that movie got me in my feelings and I don't like that," Yasmine joked while wiping her eyes acting like she was wiping actual tears. She always had this fuck niggas mentality. Which I don't blame her because they all bring trouble, but I knew she wasn't going to be like that for too long. Somebody was going to grab her ass up one day and I couldn't wait to see that.

"Who's that calling?" I asked Candy about my ringing phone.

"I don't know the number is not saved," she replied passing me my phone.

That was weird because I usually don't have random numbers calling my phone.

"Hello?" I answered.

"Are you still coming, or you just told me that because it sounded good?" the caller asked.

"Huh? Who is this?"

"Well how many people you lied to within a week?" The caller questioned.

"No one. Sorry you have the wrong number," I said and hung up.

"Who was that?" Yasmine asked.

"Girl, I don't know somebody playing games on my phone."

"Well, let me call the number back because I got time today!" Yasmine said always being so aggressive.

She grabbed my phone and sat next to me on my sofa. Sipping some more Wine, she pressed the number on my phone screen and put the phone on speaker.

"Found out who it is you lied to recently?" we heard the caller ask.

"Who is this playing games on my friend phone like we not grown?" Yasmine asked.

"Playing? I'm a grown ass man and I don't play games," the caller said agitated as if we were the ones playing the phone games.

"Who are you looking for?" Yasmine asked.

"Ms. Emerald," the caller answered.

Ms. Emerald? Only one person called me that lately. It couldn't have been him. No way has gotten a hold of my personal number. I grabbed my phone from Yasmine.

"Hello? Hello? Is this Trey?" I asked.

"Trey? Who is that?" Candy asked. I put my finger to my mouth signaling her to be quiet.

"Yeah liar."

"How did you get my number? I didn't give you my number," I asked confused. *I know I didn't give him my number.*

"I have my ways," he replied.

"Ways?!" I yelled into the phone.

"Yeah WAYS! So how many more people you lied to this week?" he questioned again.

"Lied, what did I lie to you about?"

"So, you don't remember you saying you was going to come to the barbecue?"

"Ohhhh, ummm yeah about that. I just got tied up in something," I lied. I didn't intentionally forget about the barbecue, but I didn't care to remember. I barely knew this guy. I could feel Yasmine and Candy staring, burning a hole right through me confused on what was going on.

"So, you not coming? Put your friend back on the phone," he told me obviously not asking.

"Em who is that?!" Candy yelled out and asked right after she saw me put the phone on mute.

"Okay so it's a client that I sold a home to and I don't even know how he got a hold of my number and I just—". Before I can finish talking, I heard Trey talking into the phone.

Candy grabbed my phone and took it off mute.

"Yes?" She answered.

"So, are y'all coming? Or what?" Trey asked.

"Yeah send the address," of course Candy answered.

"No!" I yelled trying to grab my phone. Yasmine put her hand over my mouth as Candy hung up the phone.

"Stop being so dramatic. We are sitting home on a weekend moping watching tearjerker movies. What's wrong with free food anyway?" Candy asked. I just looked at her because I had nothing to say.

"Exactly. We don't even have to stay long," Candy said.

"Fine whatever."

I got a text message. I knew that had to be Trey.

"132 Cluster Ave," Candy said out loud reading the message.

"Who's driving because I'm not?" I asked with an attitude.

I wasn't going to be the driver to a place I didn't even want to go.

"I'll drive, so you wouldn't have to look for parking on the way back. See how good of a friend I am," Candy said.

Yeah okay, she just wanted to go to that Barbecue.

Candace

    We been here at the barbecue for a while and it was cool. When we first got here Emerald was acting scary but loosened up after a while and I knew exactly why. What she forgot to mention was that Mr. Trey was a good-looking guy and I knew that's what her had shaken up in the first place blaming it on being unprofessional because it was a client. He just asked her to attend a barbecue, not a date! Anyways, they seemed to be kicking it off so maybe coming here wasn't a bad idea.

    I knew my eyes wasn't playing tricks on me or maybe it was. I had a drink or two nothing major, but I knew it was him. I only saw him one time but that was a face I could never forget. I saw him walking inside of the house, so I followed him. I never learn my lesson. He was on the phone and it sounded like business he was talking. He looked a little intoxicated too. He was slipping badly because he didn't even know I was following him. Hell, I didn't even know why I was following him. The house lights were dimmed so I was able to still see his every move. He went to the bar to go pour him another drink after he hung up the phone. Putting my drink on the table I slowly crept behind him and put my hands gently around his eyes. I knew he was clueless as to who it was.

"Devil in a red shirt," I whispered into his ears.

Coincidentally he had on a red shirt. Nasir grabbed my hands and turned around.

"Who the fuck?"

Focusing his eyes, I guess he was trying to see who I was.

"Candy?" He asked. Finally dawning to him. "What the fuck? You stalking me? How the hell you get in here?" This fool had the nerve to be looking like he was serious too!

Embarrassed was the only feeling I felt. What the fuck was he thinking?

"Stalking you? Excuse me? I was invited here!" I yelled.

"Invited by whom because I damn sure didn't invite you."

I was starting to get a little scared now because he really thought I was stalking him. He just ruined the whole mood. Here I was happy to see his fine ass and of course he's a lame. Just my luck! I started to walk away with him following me. Walking past a bathroom he grabbed my arm.

"Who you here with?" He asked sternly.

Rolling my eyes, I replied, "My friend Emerald came to see Trey."

"How I know you're telling the truth?" he asked.

Putting my hands up, I was getting fed up now.

"So how about you fucking go ask him!" I yelled trying to walk away just for him to grab my arm again.

"Sorry, I was just shocked to see you. I'm a most wanted man out here in these streets. I got to dodge a few stalkers here and there," he laughed literally dodging. How the fuck he goes from a crazy maniac to making jokes that quick?

"Ummm hmm," I replied crossing my arms across my chest.

"Wait? Why you so big and bold now? Just last week you were shaking in your shoes when I saw you," he laughed trying to clown me.

"Well it was dark, and you are kind of big."

"Big? You are calling me fat?" He asked.

"No, like big in a sexy way."

"Oh. So, you are calling me sexy?" He asked eyeing me as we both started laughing.

"You aightttt," I laughed.

He put his hand over his chest as if what I said hurt his feelings. This man knew he was fine, but I wasn't going to be the one to tell him. At least just not yet.

"So, who *you* came to see here?" he asked emphasizing on you.

"Nobody just tagged along with my friend. Me and the girls are about to get out of here. It was nice seeing you. Maybe we'll bump into each other another time," I said as I walked away just to get pulled back by him again. This time when he pulled me close, it was too close. The same cologne he had on that night in the club was the same one he had on now. I felt my knees getting weak from his scent and being so close to his masculine frame.

"We don't have time for maybes," he said staring into my eyes. Passing me his phone, I didn't even try to deny nor reject. I stored my number right in his phone and passed it back to him. My phone started to ring in my purse but stopped. I guess he was trying to see if I gave him the right number.

"Are you single?" he asked me.

"Yes," I replied

"Not somebody as sweet as you," he laughed, most likely referring to my name being Candy.

"Ha, very funny," I replied.

"What are you crazy or something?" he asked.

"Oh, I see you're just a jokester huh?" I asked.

Grabbing my hand, he led the way to a couch for us to sit down.

"I just want to see what I'm about to get myself into, that's all," he replied.

"About to get into?" I asked him.

"Yeah I'm interested in what I see, might be a little stalker but I think I can get past that," he laughed showing off those beautiful dimples.

"What you are drinking?" he asked me referring to the cup I had in my hand.

"A margarita," I replied. He took my cup and went to the bar and refilled it.

"Thank you," I told when he passed me back my cup.

We were sitting down maybe for an hour just getting to know one another. He seemed like a cool guy, but I didn't want to get my hopes up from just our first time really speaking.

"Hold on Candy I got to take this call," he told me getting up walking to the back. After about five minutes he came back to sit on the couch. "Unfortunately, I have to go handle some business even though I wish we can talk some more," he told me sadly as if he didn't want to go.

"Can I kiss you?" He asked me bluntly.

What! This man just went from crazy, to funny, to just insane! I was stuck with my mouth wide opened.

"Well can I?" He asked this time pulling me closer to him. We were now body to body. Both of his hands found its way around my neck as he gave me a peck on my lips. Pulling away he looked me into my eyes, I guess to see if I was going to let him proceed and I damn sure did! Coming back closer Nasir kissed me again this time biting my lip too. I knew I should've pulled away but a part of me didn't want to.

"When I call you, I'm expecting you to answer," he said and walked away. Leaving me in who knows home with some wet draws.

It was something about Nasir that had him on my mind all the time. I didn't know if it was how mysterious he was or the way he carried himself. Maybe it was the way he planted his lips onto mines like they belonged there. It was just something about him that had me. I was kind of intrigued by him with just the only two encounters we had. That's why I've been waiting so damn long for him to call me. I thought maybe he forgotten about me or didn't care to call. I thought he was going to call me that exact night of the barbecue, but here it is almost two weeks later and no call. Every time my phone would ring, I would rush to answer it thinking it's him. Imagine my disappointment over and over that it wasn't. Oh well, it wouldn't be the first time a guy said he's going to call me and don't and with my history with relationships, I don't need to be thinking about no man.

Tonight Yasmine, Emerald and I was going to a bar to let off some steam for the weekend and take as many shots as we could before going home lonely. Well Yasmine and I . I knew Trey and Nas were cool and I desperately wanted to ask Emerald to ask Trey about Nas whereabouts. But hey, the same way I could do that he can too. He told me he was going to call me, not the other way around.

We were on our fourth shot of tequila. We decided to just go to a local bar in the neighborhood, not really in the mood to go clubbing. Well not Emerald and I but Yasmine, was always ready for a club or two. It wasn't too crowded or too empty so that was always a good thing. My phone started to ring and I couldn't really hear the caller, so I went outside the bar.

"Hello?" I spoke into my phone.

"Why you not at home waiting on me?" the caller asked.

"Excuse me?"

"It's Nas."

The nerve of this fool, I thought.

"I don't know a Nas, lose my number," I said into the phone and hung up.

After I been waiting on his damn phone call for more than a week, he wants to finally decide to call me. Yeah okay, he got the wrong bitch on the right day.

Walking back into the club I saw Yasmine talking to a guy at the bar, probably getting him to buy her a drink. Emerald was sitting there looking like the happiest girl in the world texting on her phone most likely talking to Trey. I went towards to bar where Yasmine was sitting as I overheard her conversation with the guy.

"I give you my number if you buy me and my girls a drink," she said.

For one I didn't even ask her to get us another drink.

"A Margarita please," I said. *Hey why not? Shit if he is buying, I want to make sure it's right.*

"Oh, so this is one of your friends? Hello beautiful," He said shaking my hand.

Ew! He was so ugly, and I knew with him just being in Yasmine presence had him feeling like the man. He should have known he was getting played from the gate. Yasmine started to look at me like something was wrong. Trying to read her eyes, I couldn't understand.

"Why you are looking at me like that?" I asked her.

Before she can answer that familiar scent that I thought about for the last two weeks filled my nose. I felt hands gripping my waist

"Again, why you not at home waiting on me?" he asked me.

It was him.

He was so close to me I felt his breathe on my skin.

"Why would I be home waiting on something that's not mines?" I asked him.

"Oh, so that's how you feel?" Nas asked me.

"Yeah that's how I feel. Don't think after a few weeks you can just resurface. I'm a grown woman and don't have time for games."

He grabbed me and turned me around. Grabbing my chin and forcing me to look into his eyes.

"Do I look like the type of nigga to be playing games?" he asked me. His voice was so calming.

No baby! No, you don't! I thought to myself.

"Looks can be deceiving," Instead I said out of my mouth.

I saw Emerald sitting on Trey lap with him whispering in her ear. *Damn she should've warned me that they were coming.*

"No, you look, I'm not the type of man to even do this. When I first saw you, you caught my attention which is hard to even happen. Not on some love at first sight shit but I wanted to get to know more of you. Then the time after that I saw you and I had something to take care of. This time around, I wanted to give you my undivided attention. I want to learn your likes, dislikes, everything Candy. So, my fault if I had you waiting but you know how it goes, good things comes to those who wait." He grabbed my hand and kissed it. *How can somebody as fine as him be so sweet?*

"Are you playing with me?"

"You tell me what you think?" he asked me looking into my eyes. His stare was so damn strong, it felt like he can see right through me.

"Actions speak louder than words," I replied rolling my eyes. Yeah, my feelings were hurt and I didn't even know why. I didn't know this dude, but I felt something more than the usual. From the talk that we had, the way the vibes were just flowing. Nothing felt force. I thought it was a mutual feeling, but over the past two weeks, I realized it wasn't

"No seriously Candy, with the club shit going on and trying to open a new one it's a lot to handle at times and especially when everybody isn't on their A game," he said.

"Club? Oh, you're a club owner that's cool."

"Yeah the club you were roaming around looking for the *bathroom*. That's my club," he emphasized on bathroom.

"No, I really was looking for the bathroom," I laughed. "Oh, so you're the club owner that all your workers were plotting on. Hmmm," I said giving him the side eye.

"Plotting on me? Nah," he shook his head answering his own question.

"Don't be so gullible. They want you."

"Well none of that matters because the one I want is standing right in front of me," he said running his index finger up and down the side of my face.

Shit. I don't know if he was trying to turn me on or not but it damn sure was working. From what he was saying, to how he was saying it. I was ready to trade it all right here, right now!

"So, what you are waiting for?" I asked him.

"Wait, I just need to know one thing, can you cook?"

Hell no I couldn't cook but, I wasn't going to tell him that.

"Of course, I can cook. How dare you?"

"I'm just saying, I'm a man that like to eat," he winked at me.

"I love a man that like to eat," I flirted back.

Shortly after it was starting to get late and everybody was saying their goodbyes. I didn't want to leave Nas and I guess he felt the same way too because when he dropped me off home and we stayed in his car and we talked for a while. He tried to get himself into my house more than a few times, but I wasn't having it. Me alone with him? There wasn't no telling what would of, could of, and should have gone down.

"Wednesday be ready at six thirty," he said.

"What's at six thirty?" I asked him.

"I want to spend time with you," he replied looking into my eyes.

"Who said I wasn't busy?"

"Me."

"Don't be thinking you're going to be out here controlling me," I told him

"Nah ma, never that. We a team baby. You don't want to spend time with me?" He asked me.

"Yessss," I couldn't help but blush.

"So, stop running and let me in," he replied and started to rub up and down my thigh. I wanted to let him in alright. Our sexual connection was just too strong. I needed to get out of his car fast because he was starting to remind me of my jeep, like R.Kelly said.

"Well I'll see you on Wednesday," I told him trying to hurry out the car. He grabbed my hand pulling me back.

"That's how you leave me hanging?" He asked.

I leaned over and gave him a peck and jumped out the car rushing to the front of my door, tripping over my foot. I heard him laughing. I knew I probably looked like a fool but so what, he made me entirely too nervous.

"Goodnight Nas," I waved to him while he just smiled back at me and blew me a kiss. Finally, inside I closed my door and locked it. Putting my back against the wall I finally felt more relaxed. It felt like I was holding on to my breathe forever.

Shit, I think I'm in love.

Candace

"How does this look?" I asked Emerald on face time.

Today was the day me and Nas were finally going out. If I wasn't nervous before, I was nervous now.

"You look sexy. He's not going to get enough of you tonight!" She laughed.

"Where are you guys even going?" She asked.

"He didn't even tell me!" I screamed nervously.

"Maybe out to eat," Emerald suggested.

I had on a black fitted jumpsuit. The front of it was a V line that my chest looked perfect in. Of course, it wouldn't be me if I didn't show a little skin. On my feet I had on one of my favorite sandals. My black Louis Vuitton strap sandals. I looked sexy, but still casual. I didn't know where our destination was going to be so I tried to wear something that can fit in for any occasion. Just when I was about to go in my bathroom to do my makeup my phone beeped indicating another caller was trying to get through the line. I saw it was Nas, so I told Emerald I was going to call her back.

"Hello?" I spoke into the phone.

"Are you ready?" Nas asked.

"Ummmmm no. I have to do my makeup," I told him

"Makeup? What you need make up for?" He asked me.

"To look nice," I laughed

"Well I don't want you to wear no makeup tonight."

"It's going to be light you won't even notice," I whined.

"Wear any makeup and I'm going to throw some water on your face," he laughed.

"Nigga I dare you!"

"I'm just saying baby, you beautiful you don't need that," he complimented me.

"Aww thank you, you not to bad yourself," I laughed.

"Fineeee, just some mascara and lip gloss I promise."

"Okay good because I'm five minutes away," he said.

"Nas! You said six thirty!"

"I know, I know. I was getting impatient. A nigga misses you," he smiled showing those cute ass dimples.

"I miss you too Nasir," I smiled into the phone.

Shortly after he told me he was here and to come down. When I got outside. Being the gentleman, he was, he stood by the passenger door with a bouquet of red roses in his hand.

"You look beautiful," he told me and kissed me on the cheek handing me the roses. I knew I had a big smile on my face because my cheeks were starting to hurt. I couldn't help it.

"And you look handsome."

He had on a white button up with some navy-blue jeans. On his feet was a pair of Gucci sneakers. He looked casual but in a sexy way. After I got into his Navy-Blue Mercedes Benz, he came around the car and got in the driver's seat.

"So where are we going?" I asked him.

"It's a surprise," he replied.

"We're here," Nas said.

I looked around and realized we were at a park. I was so into our conversation like always. I didn't even notice that the car was parked.

"A park?" I asked him confused getting out of the car.

"Yup, a park," he said. Grabbing my hand, we walked deeper into the park.

"Interesting choice," I nodded.

"Yeah I was trying to be out the box. I wanted something more intimate with nobody around to distract us. Just me and you." I don't know how I lucked up with this man. Now that I think about it, I realized this was the most romantic thing anyone has ever done for me.

I noticed a big white sheet with red rose petals in the shape of a heart. More rose petals surrounded the sheet. He also had candles set up that I pray didn't fall over. The sun was setting so this scene looked more beautiful than ever. Also, a picnic basket I can smell the food from that smelled so good.

"So, what do you think?" He asked. He knew this was beautiful but of course he wanted to gloat and hear it himself.

"You did all of this for me?" I grabbed his face and kissed him. "Thank you, baby," I squealed as he blushed showing off those beautiful dimples that I adored. I honestly did love it. I never had experienced anything like this ever before. I took off my shoes before getting on the sheet to sit down as he did the same.

"So, what's on the menu?" I knew we were having some type of meal, so I purposely didn't eat a lot today.

"Well we got some salad, fish, pasta, chicken, we got it all baby," he laughed.

"It looks so good too, where did you get this from?" I asked as I made our plates.

"I asked my mother to hook me up," He replied staring at me like I was the meal he was about to devour.

"She did all of this for you? That's nice," I replied.

Shit! I hope he don't think I can be busting meals out like this. My cooking skills are nowhere near this, I thought.

"Yeah one day maybe you can do her hair at the salon," he said.

"Not yet, it's too soon I'm scared," I laughed.

"Scared of what baby? Y'all going to have to meet one day being that you're going to be the one to give her some grandchildren," he winked.

"Kids?" I asked.

"Yeah kids, you don't want any?" He pressed.

"Ummm kids just really wasn't something heavily on my mind," I replied.

Of course, I wanted kids! But with all the fertility issues I had in the past, kids were far from my mind. I didn't want to scare him away and tell him about that. It's way too soon. Who knows where this would even go?

"Oh okay, maybe I can change that for you," he grabbed my hand and kissed it.

I'm pretty sure nobody can change it, I thought.

"Why do you look so sad suddenly? About having kids. Look Candy, I'm not saying anytime soon. This is our time to make us better than ever. Nothing is rushed baby, I would never force anything on you," He said starring in my eyes like he can see right into my soul.

Only if he knew, I thought.

"Yes, baby I know," I told him.

Changing the subject because I didn't want to be the downfall of our date, I brought up his clubs and asked him more about the ideas for his new one as we ate our meal.

After finishing our food, we lay on the sheet and stared into the stars. It was now pitch-black outside. I told him we should go because it was getting late, but he reassured me that he wasn't that nigga to play with and if he says we good, we're good.

"You know your sexy right," I told him rubbing the side of his face.

"Here you go trying to run some game on me," he laughed.

"That's all from right here," I grabbed his hand and put it on my heart. Of course, it wouldn't be Nas if he didn't change a sweet moment into something nasty.

"You mean right here?" He asked as he grabbed my left breast.

"No, nasty!" I laughed slapping his hand away.

"Nah I'm playing baby. You just can't have me out here blushing and shit. Making me look soft," he laughed.

"Oh, I'm sorry. I forgot you the big bad wolf. My fault homie," I joked.

He grabbed my face and kissed me with those irresistible lips.

"Did you enjoy yourself?" He asked.

"Anytime I get to spend with you is enjoyable," I replied.

"Okay mac I see you," he laughed.

I wouldn't trade this moment for nothing in the world.

Emerald

Two months later...

"Hey Mr. Forest," I giggled into the phone.

"What I told you about calling me that?" Trey asked.

He hated when I called him by his last name. I thought it was cute.

"Oh, I'm sorry heyyyy daddy," I purred.

"Stop playing before I really be having you calling me daddy," he chuckled.

He still never told me how he got a hold of my personal number but after the barbecue everything just flowed. We're basically in a relationship but neither one of us put a title on it. I noticed how he would get upset if a guy looked at me too hard or if I tell him about an incident when a guy tried to flirt with me, so I stopped it overall. I told him he didn't have anything to worry about, but he wasn't having that.

"What time do you think I should be ready by?" I asked him. We were supposed to be going to dinner.

"Don't be mad at me baby."

"What happened now?"

"Something came up now I'm on my way to handle it with Maine," he explained.

"Okay Trey," I said rolling my eyes.

It was always something. He told me I knew the kind of life he lived but damn! People make time for the things they cared about!

"Aww don't be like that baby. I promise I'll make it up you," he said.

"Whatever."

"I'm going to call you as soon as I'm done baby."

"Yeah okay," I said hanging up the phone.

Grabbing my phone, I texted my coworker and took him up on his offer to the movies. Better than sitting home waiting on Trey until whatever time in the morning.

Trey

    Ever since Nas left the game on some pussy shit, I've had to prove myself even more to these niggas. Don't get it confused though, I'm that nigga out here in these streets. But, two was always better than one. Me and Nas came up together in this game. We started from nothing to something. Growing up where we came from its either you got a killer jump shot or you going to be in them streets making money. Shit I prefer this way even more. I got the money, the fucking respect and the bitches. Can't beat that. Money making niggas out here. Then, suddenly nigga started seeing a different light in life. Walking around in suits and owning clubs on some Ghost from Power shit. Might as well start his own TV show. He tried to get me into that but nah that's not how I want to live my life. I love the adrenaline this shit gives me. With him out the picture that's where my nigga Maine came into place. He was the next runner up so why the fuck not? I wasn't really fucking with Nas like that anyway. Nigga might be wearing a wire or some shit. How we go from leaving the city a mess to him wanting to go legit? Shit seem weird to me. That's still my nigga, just from afar. You never really know what niggas motives be now and days.

"Yo come downstairs," I spoke into the phone.

"I'm already on it," Maine replied.

We were on our way to make an example out of niggas. Don't come up short with my shit! I don't know how many times I have to say that, but now I was done talking. I said it enough already.

Maine got in the car and we were on our way. He already had a blunt rolled too. That's why he was my nigga!

It took us a little minute to get there but I was relaxed now. That weed had me feeling a little calmer.

"Yo what's good Trey?" one of my young niggas I had working for me called out.

I got heated all over again! That fucking fast! Why the fuck niggas out here smiling and thinking shit sweet when I don't have all my fucking money? I called a meeting at one of the warehouses, so everybody was here attending. Like they better fucking be. Not the one to like to waste any of my time, I got straight to the point.

"So, who was in charge of the last count?" I asked.

I didn't get a verbal answer but everybody eyes answered the question for me.

They all looked at Shug.

Shug was my little homie from the South. When I use to go out there and do some work that's how we met. I know for a fact he knew better than to fuck with my shit. I stared at him and he knew what the fuck was going through my head, so I didn't even have to ask. He was sitting there shaking like a stripper trembling and shit, so I already knew what was up.

"You know I never come up short Trey. You came a week earlier for the pickup than usual! I would never steal from you!" He pleaded.

"So, what the fuck happened? You can't fucking count?!" I walked closer to him.

"You know my mother is sick man I just needed to pay her hospital bill and I was going to put it right back before you came to get it. You know I would never steal from you," he said.

"I knew I had to bugging. I'm over here like not my nigga Shug?" I chuckled. "How momma love doing?" I asked him walking up to him.

He seemed a little relax now.

"She good thank god. You know I would never. Thank you for understanding man," he said wiping his forehead.

The nerve of this nigga to look relief.

I couldn't even fake it any longer if I wanted to. I pulled out my gun and shot him right in his head. He didn't even see it coming. Nobody seen the shit coming.

"NOW PLAY WITH MY FUCKING MONEY AGAIN. I DONT GIVE A SHIT IF YOUR MOTHER, GRANDMOTHER, OR FUCKING DOG IS SICK! I SEE I GOTTA START MAKING EXAMPLES OUT OF NIGGAS!" I yelled looking at everybody in the fucking room.

Everyone had the look of shock on their faces.

"Now clean this shit up! I just bought these fucking shoes!" I said and walked out.

These niggas were going to learn today!

I called Emerald to find out she at the movies with her coworker. Sound like a fucking date to me. What nigga goes to the movies and don't want no fucking pussy in return? I see today is just the day that I obviously have to prove myself to everybody. She wanted to play with me. Well we were going to play today. I asked her what movies theater she was going to and what time it was over so I can meet her at my spot. She still had her place but most of the time she would be at my spot instead. Well I fucking lied. I was parked up right outside that bitch! Fuck she is doing going out to the movies anyway! We can watch a movie in the crib! The movie was over at 10:15 but I was giving her a little time to spare. Like clockwork at 10:20 I saw her walking out the movies smiling like she had the best time in the world. Some square ass nigga was behind her holding the door. It looked like they were telling each other goodnight. Well I wanted to say goodnight too. I wasn't far from the entrance, so I got out my car and walked towards them. Emerald was looking like a deer caught in headlights and square pants was just looking like a confused square ass nigga.

"Was sup baby?" I walked up to her and grabbed her ass while eyeing that bozo.

"Trey. Stop. What are you doing here?" She asked trying to pry my hands off her.

"Are you good Emerald?" The square had the nerve to ask.

"Yeah nigga she good!" I told him.

"Yes, goodnight Mason," she told him.

"Figures," I laughed.

A square ass name for a square ass dude.

"Figures?" He had the nerve to ask.

"Yeah nigga figures!" I said walking up to him.

Oh, I get it, he was trying to show off for Emerald. I spot niggas like him from a mile away. He wanted to show off, so I was going to give him exactly what he wanted. He was posted up like he wanted to do something.

"Problem?" I asked him.

"Do you have a problem?" He asked me back.

I was already still on one after the meeting and this shit wasn't making it any better. He was doing too much talking for me, so I walked up to him pulled my gun out and knocked him right upside his head with it. He fell to the floor with blood leaking from his head, getting on my fucking shoes again!

"Sorry man! I was just making sure the lady was good," he pleaded.

Exactly what I thought.

"Trey! What are you doing? You're going to go to jail let's go!" Emerald cried. *Fuck is she crying for this nigga for?*

"Mason I'm so sorry, please," she cried.

Now she was apologizing to this cornball.

She was grabbing my arm pulling me towards my car with tears coming down her face. I put my gun back in my waist and smiled. I bet her ass will think twice about going to the fucking movies again.

Nas

Yasir was acting like he didn't want to drop his own damn brother home. I knew I should've bought my car, but the nigga insisted on letting him drive now suddenly, he got something to do. I would've called a lyft but why do that when I can make a reason to see Candy. I've been busy with the club and she been busy working at the salon. I loved the motivation she had because these females be lazy as hell!

"Baby, what you are doing?" I asked her. She was still playing games scared to be alone with me but always had some slick shit to say.

"Nothing I was just thinking about you," she replied.

"Oh really? What about me?" I asked her.

"Nothing I just miss you," she laughed.

"You do? So, come get me," I told her.

"Your car broke down big guy?" She laughed.

"No smart ass. My punk ass brother flaked on me after he the one who dropped me off at the club," I explained. "Or I can just get one of the workers here to drop me off," I added.

I knew that was going to get to her. She disliked the ones she claims be giving me the eye.

"Nas, don't play with me... Matter of fact I dare you," she replied and hung up.

I was starting to know Candy like the back of my hand, so I knew she was coming. I took care of a few things just to kill time before she got here.

About a half an hour later Candy texted me and told me to come outside. I told everybody goodnight before I proceeded walking towards the front of the club.

"You came just in time one of them just offered me a ride," I teased her as I got in the car.

She pulled off fast as lightning and my head jerked back before I can even put on my seat belt.

"Candy you play to damn much!" I yelled at her. She always went to the extreme with her dramatic ass.

"Oops my bad," she laughed.

Having small talk as she drove the car, I decided to start fucking with her.

"Who you looking all good for? Where were you going?" I asked her.

"Look good? Baby I just threw this on to come get you," she laughed.

She knew what the hell she was doing. She had on a tight ass dress that she better had only worn in the fucking house. I could see the imprint of her damn nipples and every curve on her body. I grabbed the dress and ripped it on the side until it got to her waist exposing her thighs more.

"Nas! Why would you do that? I love this dress!" she yelled.

"Because I don't want anybody else seeing you in it."

Yeah, the dress looked nice but fuck it. I can buy her as many of the same dresses that she wanted. Right now, I honestly didn't want her to have shit on. I was tired of waiting to get a feel of what was mines. I know women liked to wait and get a feel of the dude first. Fuck that! I was as real as it gets. I knew it had to be something else holding her back because the look in her eyes showed me that she wanted me too. I was taking it slow with her, but I didn't know how long I can last. Candy was a woman that liked to show off her sex appeal, which I had no problem with because I wasn't an insecure dude. I just didn't know how many nights I could go to sleep with blue balls I had left in me. I started to rub on her thighs moving my fingers closer to her inner thigh.

"Nas what are you doing?"

She tried to hit my hand away.

"Keep your hands on the wheel before you kill us," I told her.

I finally got to her pussy and grabbed her thong and ripped it off stuffing them in my pocket. She was staring at the road not looking paranoid as hell. I started to rub on her clit slowly.

"Nas, stop," she said.

"Why? It doesn't feel good?" I asked her.

"I'm driving!" She yelled.

"Well you better do a good damn job at it," I laughed as she rolled her eyes.

I got closer to her, putting one of my fingers inside of her while rubbing on her clit. Her cheeks started to flush. Her pussy was wetting up my fingers real fast. I put another one inside. Her pussy felt so tight; I can just imagine how that shit would feel wrapped around my dick.

"Nas you about to make me cum," she moaned.

I went a little faster and felt her pussy pulsating as she came on my fingers. She looked embarrassed because she came so fast. If I could make her cum that fast with my fingers shit imagine what I can do with my dick.

At the same time, she stopped the car, I pulled my fingers out and put them to her mouth as she licked her essence off. She grabbed my head and kissed me so I can taste her. She tasted just how I imagined. She got out of the car and walked to my gate and I followed behind her.

"Baby I just asked you to drop me off you didn't have to come inside. I know you scared to get past the door. I could come over tonight if you want." I told her after entering my gate.

"Oh, what you thought you was going to do all that and not give me any dick?" She asked.

I thought she was going to start laughing but she was serious. Shit, if she wanted the dick. The dick is what I was going to give her.

Candace

I tried. I really did try. I think this was the hardest thing I ever had to do. To resist Nas sexy ass. At the club when I first saw him and at the barbecue, both times I was ready to give it all to him. I didn't know if he would look at me different if I gave it up so quick, so I always had to get my mind right every time he came around. The fight between what my mind thought was right and what my body felt I needed, was becoming overbearing. He's been taking it slow with me. Respecting how I felt and that made me what to give it to him even more.

"You sure you ready with all that big talk you are doing?" He asked me.

I'm pretty sure he thought I was joking around.

"You got to promise me you won't be going all crazy and shit after," He laughed.

"Boy please."

"Okay but I'm warning you."

This was the first time I've been inside of his house. Every time he tried to get me to come in, I would make him drive me home. It was something about him that was intimidating, and I knew after we had sex there wasn't any turning back. But tonight, I couldn't resist it. It was like he was so perfect I wouldn't want sex to change anything between us. The vibe he was giving me wasn't anything compared to that but sometimes you just never know.

His house was beautiful. Walking inside, the scenery felt like a lot of money was put into his home. The living room was all white with not one touch of black. From the couches to the rug. The center piece table was an aqua blue thick glass piece. The vibe of the living room gave off a cold, cozy winter night I didn't even want to walk towards the living room scared that my shoes might get the rug dirty. It looked like one of those places that you can look but can't touch. I immediately took my shoes off. Walking more into the house I saw the kitchen. He got behind the bar and offered me a drink.

"Some wine would be okay," I requested.

"Wine? Sorry baby I only got some Cognac right about now unless you want some Vodka or Heinekens?"

"D'usse?"

"You just got lucky," he said grabbing the bottle from behind the bar. I liked that liquor because it went down smoothly.

"A shot to us and the future," he said pouring the shot.

And I happily took the shot with him. Whatever it was that we were doing felt so right, I knew it couldn't be wrong.

Two hours later with the bottle being almost done, Chris Brown "Privacy" was playing on the radio and he was performing for me. Looking sexy but like a fool. I couldn't help but to keep laughing, he was on beat though, I give him that.

"I was originally supposed to be one of those singers that get crazy on the dance floor," he said.

"Of course, Nas."

"You don't believe me? Okay watch this," Walking towards me grabbing my hand leading me up the stairs. He walked passed two doors and then he opened the door to one of them. Inside was the biggest bed I've ever seen in my life. Most likely he got it custom made. The bed had burgundy satin sheets on it. The room gave me sort of like a cabin vibe. It was like each room in his home had a different look to it. Nothing was similar.

"Hold on, I'll be back," He said and went into another door in his room, I'm guessing the bathroom. The lights in the room automatically dimmed down. *What was he up to now?* Now I was getting nervous.

He came out of the bathroom with a white towel wrapped around his waist. I automatically looked down at his print and my eyes got big ass saucers. *All of that was supposed to fit in me.* He must have noticed because he started to chuckle. I was sitting in the middle of the bed and he started to walk towards me singing Feenin by Jodeci as it played in the background.

All the chronic in the world couldn't even mess with you.
You're the ultimate high.
You hear what I'm saying, baby?

Oh, so this is what he meant by performing. He came to me and grabbed my hand and put it on the outline of his dick. I felt it throbbing. I tried to grab it but then he pushed my hand away. He grabbed my hand and turned me around. Grabbing my breast, he caressed both. His hands started to go lower and lower until he got to my ass. He bent down and bit it, then kissed it. Pain and then pleasure. I started to take off my dress, well was barely left of it after he ripped it, but he stopped me.

"We not in a rush, let me take my time," He whispered in my ear. I felt him drop his towel. He grabbed my waist and started to rotate it on his dick.

"You finally ready to give me what's mines?" He asked me.

"I been ready," I told him.

"Oh really?" He chuckled.

He turned me back around and I swear his dick was the prettiest dick I've ever seen in my life. I tried to grab it again but then he pushed me down on the bed and got on top me and started singing in my ear.

I don't mind.
It's all on you, baby.
Girl, I'm so strung out.
All I do is wish for you.
So, tomorrow if you're not here,
then girl, I'm down, so I need you near.

I was so into him I forgot he put the song on. He sounded so good and was turning me on so much I knew it was a wet spot right under me. He grabbed my dress and pulled it above my head. *Thank god*, I thought. Ripping a piece of my dress off he tied it around my eyes and told me he was going to be right back.

A few minutes later I felt his energy in the room, so I knew he was back already. Just feeling his energy had me hot. I wanted to pull this piece of cloth off my face, but I was curious to feel what he had next in store for me. My breathing started to speed up once his hands touched my body. I felt him opening my legs. I couldn't see him, so I didn't know what was next. All I could do was wait until he was ready to explore my body. The kisses started from my feet first until he reached higher and higher making his way to my hidden treasure. Feeling his warm breath face to face with it, I wanted to grab his head to speed up the process. Feeling my juices ease its way out of me, I couldn't take it anymore. The buildup, the wait, I needed Nas to put this fire out now. I don't know why he wanted to tease me.

"You want me to kiss it?" He asked.

"Yes Nas, pleaseee," I begged.

"You never going to keep it away from me this long again?" He asked.

"I promiseeee," I told him. He had me making promises and shit and I didn't even get the dick yet. Suddenly, I felt his mouth on me and it felt so good. I felt like I was about to cum already.

"Relax," He said with a mouthful of my pussy in his mouth. *Why was he telling me to relax?* I had no control over my body.

Right after I felt something cold going inside of me. I'm guessing a piece of ice. I tried to push him away, but he grabbed both of my wrist as the ice slide out of me. "Don't move," he told me. Placing the ice in his mouth he started doing things I would've never imagined with it. I never had this done to me and I couldn't even explain the feeling. It was a foreign feeling but then again it felt so good. I was already Cumming in his mouth. He started moaning too, so I guess he was enjoying it himself. Shortly after, still left without eyesight, I heard him opening a condom to put it on.

"Wait, Nas it hurts," I told him once I felt him pushing his was into me.

"I thought you was ready for it?" He asked.

Shit, I thought I was too.

He grabbed my breast and started kissing on them. He started to suck on my nipple while massaging the other one going inch by inch inside of my pussy. He grabbed both of my breast licking both of my nipples at the same time. I never even knew that was possible. Finally, all of him was inside of me.

"Damn Candy," He moaned into my ear.

Damn was right because that's the same thing I was thinking.

Stroking slowly taking his time, I felt him sucking all over my neck. My legs started to shake as I came on his dick already. He revealed my eyes and I finally saw him. Ugh! He was the sexiest man I ever laid eyes on. The faces he was making was so sexy. I couldn't even talk or stop moaning. Sex never felt like this to me.

"Baby can I feel you without the condom?" he moaned in my ear. I wasn't on my birth control, so I wasn't trying to have any slip ups.

"No, Nas," I moaned.

"I promise I'm going to pull out," he said stroking faster and faster as I came on his dick again. He pulled out of me and took the condom off.

"Baby, oh my goddd," I moaned as he put his dick back inside of me. I don't know how it was possible that it felt better than before, and this was the best dick I ever felt in my life. I grabbed the back of his head pulling him towards me and kissed him while grinding back on his dick.

"This my pussy?" He asked me.

"Yes, baby it's all yours," I moaned.

"It better fucking be," He grunted.

He was hitting spots I didn't even know existed. I lost track of how many times he made me cum but after two hours I was drained, and he still wanted more. I had to beg him for us to take a break. Once he agreed I knocked right out. Now I knew why he told me don't get crazy. Sorry to say the damage was already done after what he did to me. That ass was mines!

Nas decided to randomly tell me he wanted a home cook meal. Now when I first met him, I told him I could cook, only because he caught me off guard. I'm not the worst cook, but I'm damn sure not the best. I'm just always busy and never really had time to sit and learn. Well today was going to be the day something happened. I honestly wanted to go to a soul food place and buy some pans, but Yasmine and Emerald thought I should just do it and go for it.

So here I was at seven in the afternoon beating pots and pans in a kitchen that I barely even used. The food didn't look too bad or smell bad and I re-read everything from on the internet over and over. I made him some Steak, Macaroni and Cheese, Baked Potatoes, and some Sautéed Shrimp. He texted me and told me he was on his way, so I decided to just hurry and set the table.

****

Nas took a bite of the steak I made with a smile on his face. A nervous smile. *Shit! I knew I fucked up.*

"A little tough just like your man," he laughed.

Was he trying to make a joke about my Steak?

"Baby do you like it?" I questioned.

With each bite he took off his plate I kept questioning him. I knew it wasn't what he was used to because his mother can throw down. He just kept nodding his head and telling me it was good. I knew he was lying. I wish he would just tell me the truth already. *If it was so damn good, why is it even still food on his plate?* I saw Nas chow food down and finish a whole plate within ten minutes. It was now after ten and he still had a plate of food. I knew something was wrong, I just wish he would admit it.

"Come here Candy," He said.

I walked over to him and sat on his lap.

He brushed my hair from the front of my face and gave me a kiss on my cheek. I know I looked a hot mess and exhausted. Cooking was not the easiest thing to do. I had stains all over my clothes and my hair was halfway into an afro. I couldn't even get sexy before he came because like Nas, he came earlier than expected nagging me that he was hungry, so I had to make it work.

"Why you lied to me?" He asked.

Damn was it that bad? I guess he was tired of faking the funk.

"Lied? Lied about what baby?" I asked nervously.

"I thought you said you won cooking tournaments and cooked every thanksgiving for your family." I busted out laughing. Okay, I might have been just a little over dramatic.

"I didn't want you to think less of me baby. I want to be like... superwoman to you," I shrugged.

"Candy, I can never think less of you. I would've just hooked you up with my mother on Sundays. You know she loves you already," he laughed. When I first met his mother, Yvonne it was like I already knew her. Being a man of his word, he brought her to my salon without even informing me. The kicker was, he didn't walk in with her, so I had no clue she was even his mother. She finally spilled the beans revealing who she was. Nas theory was that he wanted her to meet me unexpected like he did, no pressure, so I can be one hundred percent myself and she can see exactly what he saw in me when we first met, minus the sexual attraction we have for one another.

"I don't want her thinking I can't feed her son," I pouted.

"Baby, we all got to start somewhere." I smiled deep inside because this is what I admired about him. He was never negative in any situation, always the one with an answer that may help you along the way. This was exactly what I needed because deep down, I am self-conscious about a lot.

"So, you didn't like the steak Nas?" I questioned.

"Baby that shit almost broke my tooth!" He yelled massaging his jaw. I ran to my room. I was so embarrassed.

"Baby I'm just playingggg," he laughed following me.

He came up to me and grabbed me from behind and whispered in my ear, "Baby, I would lose all my teeth just to be in your presence."

"Jerk!" I hit him across his ear.

"Can you order some Pizza or something though? I'm hungry ass shit!" he yelled walking away.

"You better be glad I love you!" I yelled.

Shit, I caught myself. We never told each other those words before. Hopefully he didn't hear me because now I was slightly embarrassed. Changing the subject, I asked him what he wanted on his pizza.

"Baby, I can't hear you!" he yelled from the bathroom.

Walking to the bathroom door, I asked him again. He insisted that he didn't hear me still. Opening, the door I covered my nose. It smelled like something died in here.

"Nas you stink! What do you want on your pizza?" I asked him covering my nose.

"Whatever you are getting baby it doesn't matter," he replied

"You know you heard me! I don't know why you called me in here!"

"Because I wanted to tell you I love you too," he said.

My heart dropped as I looked at him. I ran to him and kissed him before running out the bathroom. I knew he was going to be the man that I married.

Emerald

A few months later...

"I think I'm going to have to get on new birth control," Candy said.

"Why what's wrong?" I asked her.

"My body just don't feel the same and I know that's the reason why," she responded.

We were sitting in the backyard of Nas parents' home. I made sure I came here every Sunday to get some food. Candy kept on bragging about her food all the time, so I told her to bring me a plate. Shitttttt, that was one of the best meals I've had in my life. I loved Nas mother also. She gave all of us a motherly love and had no problem with us coming to eat her food. As much as she complained about it, she made sure to cook a big meal too so hey, I low key think she enjoyed us being here. Yasmine never really came because her and Yasir, Nas twin brother would get into it. They need to grow up, seriously.

"So, when are you going to tell Nas about the miscarriages?" I asked Candy.

She looked around before responding to make sure the close was clear.

"Never," she said.

"Candy why not?" I asked.

"You wouldn't understand," she replied looking away.

"And you still taking the birth control behind his back?" I asked her.

"Yes Em! What do you think?" She asked obviously getting upset.

When she came up with the idea to take the birth control behind his back and put it in a vitamin bottle, I thought it was a stupid idea. But with how far she has gotten with it, I now see that it's working.

"Candy, you have a man that loves you in and out and adores you. I don't see Nas not being open minded about it."

"I don't want to talk about it," she cut me off.

"Well. I'm having a baby," I told her.

"A baby??? Omg are you pregnant?" she looked at me surprised.

"No silly not yet. Trey said that he wants me to have his baby," I replied rubbing my belly.

"Oh."

"Oh? You were just so happy about it. Why the sudden change?" I asked her.

"Well I forgot Trey would be the child's father," she rolled her eyes.

"Candy? Who else?!" I asked laughing.

"Mason," she said as we both laughed

It was so wrong how Trey did him. Mason doesn't even look my way anymore. When people in the office asked what happened to his face, he says he got jumped. I let him tell that lie to keep his pride. I did miss him as a friend, but I understood how he felt.

"Emerald I just don't know about you and Trey," Candy said.

"What's wrong?" I asked.

"Well Trey is always out, and you complain about him being in the streets a lot. You think he's going to change all that for a baby?" she asked.

"Nas is always out working!" I said. I know I was getting defensive but deep down I knew what she was saying was right.

"Yes, and at the club Em. You just always complain about how you're lonely and never know what Trey is doing. If he's arrested or even alive. I just want what's best for you."

Yes, I was lonely, but I knew Trey was just out getting money. He promised me it wouldn't be that way for too long and he would start making business plans soon. It was stupid for me to think this, but in the back of my mind I felt a baby would change him.

"Buttttt, you know I would support you either way. Gommy is here!" She laughed. We always made a promise to one another we would be the godparents of each other kids no matter what.

We started to talk about baby names until Yvonne, Nas mother told us the food was ready.

Nas and Candy were being the only love birds in the corner feeding one another like always. Being around them made me get a little sad because I barely spent time with Trey, but they never made me feel like a third wheel which was great also, besides when she fed him. The food was so good of course I packed up some food for me and Trey if he was to come over tonight. Just like clockwork thinking about him, Trey texted me and told me he was coming over so make sure my ass was home. I missed my man so much, so I was going to be home waiting for his ass. After eating, we went to sit in the living room to watch some television until they disappeared.

I was sitting in the living room waiting for Candy and Nas realizing they been gone for too long. I knew damn sure they were not fucking in his mother house! You just never know with them two. If she wasn't on birth control, she would have been pregnant because they go at it like rabbits. I texted her to tell her I was leaving and heard her phone which she left on the sofa. Well, she would get my message whenever she gets back to her phone.

Walking out the door I heard what sounded like moans coming from behind the house. Really? Where his mother lived you wouldn't be able to see inside her backyard with the gates that surrounded it. They didn't have any home training or shame in their game. I texted her again telling her that she and Nas was nasty laughing as I got into my car.

When I got home, I took a shower and rubbed some vanilla scented glitter body lotion on me. Trey loved that smell on me. Lighting a few candles around the house, I put on some soft music. Trey told me he was on his way and I wanted to surprise my man. Just when I was about to go to my room, I heard his car pull up in my driveway. Walking to my front door I opened it. He looked me up and down licking his lips. I'm glad he like what he sees because I was all his. I had on a Lavender colored two-piece Lingerie set with the robe to match. The robe was long with the fur around the bottom of the sleeves and bottom of the robe. I saw it online and just had to buy it to wear for Trey.

His eyes were so low. I loved that sexy high look he always had after smoking. My man so damn fine.

"All of this for me?" He asked.

"Yes baby," I blushed.

"You know I love you right?"

He grabbed me and started to kiss on my neck grabbing my ass.

"Wait baby I wanted us to have a drink first," I told him.

"Fuck that shit."

He picked me up as I wrapped my legs around him. We made our way to the bedroom and he laid me on the bed.

"Thank you baby I appreciate it," He said kissing on my collar bone.

He laid me down looking at me like he wanted to devour me.

"You look so sexy," he said while massaging his manhood. He was turning me on so much I couldn't wait for him to put himself inside of me.

I got on my knees in the doggy style position and grabbed his dick and put it in my mouth. I moved the robe from behind me so he can have a clear view of my ass while I sucked his dick. I knew he was enjoying how it felt because he was grunting while taking control of my head movements. I started to play with myself getting turned on from pleasing him. Just as I was about to cum on my fingers, he stopped me and laid me back down.

He positioned himself inside of me. He felt so good pumping back and forth in and out of me.

"You going to give me my baby, right?" He asked.

"Yesss," I moaned.

"You not just saying that because my dick is inside or you right?"

"No, baby I promise. I'll give you whatever you want," I moaned. His dick had me gone for real. If a baby is what my man wanted, a baby was what I was going to give him.

For the first time ever, he released inside of me and I had no doubt in my mind that this was a mistake, or so I thought.

Trey

    I was starting to feel the effects of this bottle already. I told this nigga Maine I didn't come to get all fucked up just was coming to show love for his birthday. We were at a strip club named "Passion". I came here a few times here and there but really stopped coming overall because Emerald friend, Yasmine worked here and always went back and told Emerald shit in my fucking business like I'm fucking her. Her and Candy fucking asses. I was hoping I didn't see Yasmine ass tonight that's why I was in the cut. If I didn't meet Emerald first Yasmine could've gotten the dick. Shit she still can with her fine chocolate ass. They had some bad bitches in here too. Maine kept talking about this one girl name Hypnotic. I knew the bitch couldn't be that bad but shit who knows because this nigga was obviously sweating her.

"Yo there she goes!" He yelled pointing across the room as we all looked in that direction.

Damn she was bad, I'm not even going to front. She was light skin with short bright red hair that looked sexy as hell on her. Thicker than a mother fucking snicker too. She had me admiring her beauty from afar.

"Aright nigga I mentioned that one was me tonight," Maine said.

"Nigga you can have that broad. I don't want her," I said shrugging my shoulders.

Hypnotic got closer to our section and I couldn't help but stare.

"I heard we had a birthday boy here tonight," she said while looking straight at me.

"That would be me," Maine replied.

Once Maine said that she went over to him and started dancing on him. Maine was enjoying all of what she was doing to him. I was wishing that was me, and obviously she was too because she couldn't keep her eyes off me. Looking down at my phone I realized I had a few missed calls and messages from Emerald asking me when I was coming home. She stayed down my back like damn, give a nigga some space sometimes. I love her and all but a nigga still young and all that settling down shit isn't for me. She wanted to be like Candy and Nas so bad I felt like she tried to push that shit on us.

"You want a dance too?" Hypnotic asked me with pure lust in her eyes.

HELL, YEAH, I WANTED A DANCE, I thought.

But not knowing if Yasmine was here tonight, I passed her dance down. Hypnotic looked disappointed but shit I don't know this broad and was not trying to take any chances.

"Nigga you must be crazy," Rah said. He was Maine little cousin, a young wild nigga too. That's why I fucked with him.

"Nigga you crazy. I am not trying to have Emerald down my back with shit she heard when I see her."

"Ohhhhh, I forgot you a lockdown in love Nigga. Pussy! Yo hypnotic bring that fat ass over here! I want a dance!" He said flashing stacks of money out his pocket.

"Fuck that shit nigga. Yeah, I got love for her, but I am not trying to jeopardized not getting no pussy tonight nigga," I laughed.

"Yeah aight whatever you say. Pussy whipped ass nigga," he laughed.

Sasha

"This bitch done lucked up tonight!" Cinnamon said.

Cinnamon was a funny bitch, so I knew it was hating behind that comment. She was a pretty girl, so I don't know what the hate was about. Bitches in here just be mad when it's enough fucking money to go around.

"Yup, you should've been there," I laughed.

Shit, I can throw around shade too.

"Don't mind that hoe," Mia said.

Mia was my down ass bitch since the sandbox. She always been the most loyal on my team. We did it all together and here we are the badest bitches in Passion. I would never replace her. Each time bitches try to get in between us and ruin our friendship they always fail.

"Girl I made so much money up thereeeeee," I happily exclaimed.

"I saw you doing your thing girl. Did you and the birthday boy start something up?" she asked.

"Uhhhh no. He's cute and all but I had my eye on somebody else," I smiled

Trey was so fucking fine. Everybody who was somebody knew about him. Well, all of them if you asked me. They were one of the biggest getting money and most dangerous niggas around. They had they hand in every fucking illegal thing there was to be doing. I know they had the law on their payroll because it wasn't no way they be moving like that and still didn't get caught up.

"Yeah, Trey I bet right," she responded.

I thought I felt a little shade around that comment, but I could be tripping. They came here a lot but lately Trey hasn't been around, so when I saw him tonight, I thought it was going to be my chance to catch me a fly ass nigga like him. Imagine how I felt when he turned me down. I'm fucking Hypnotic! The most addicted shit in this building. Turn me down for what? The nigga must be blind because there wasn't any fucking way! I was going to keep that little embarrassment to myself.

Thinking about his fine ass had me getting a little moist. It was just something about him that had me. It could've been the bad boy vibe, the way he carried himself, or even those sexy ass hazel eyes. He was not getting out of my eyesight tonight! No matter what it is I have to do, I was getting that ass tonight!

I was leaving early just to put my plan into motion. I had a bartender bring a bottle over to their section and told her to give it just to Trey. On the receipt I wrote him a little cute request only a gay nigga would turn down.

I hope my plan worked because it was a little cold outside and I was waiting by his car. Everybody knew Trey was the only nigga riding around in a Red Mercedes Benz around the hood so of course I knew this was his car. Not trying to be too noticeable I was by a car on the side of his.

I was finally starting to lose hope because it's been about 10 minutes now. Shit well it was worth a try. I knew I should've drove my fucking car tonight.

"Hypnotic?"

I heard somebody call my name.

Turning around I saw it was Trey holding the bottle I bought for him. I can't believe it worked.

"You better practice what you preach. I don't got all day."

Oh, I sure was. They don't call me Hypnotic for any reason.

He drove us to the Marriott in Manhattan. Trey skipped the line and was automatically given a key. See, this is why I need a man like him. He ran every fucking thing. We got to the suite and he went to sit down to roll his blunt. Opening the bottle of Moët, he took some to the head and poured me glass. Cutting to the chase I asked him why he denied my dance. Yeah, I was still in my feelings about that.

"It wasn't that, my girlfriend home girl work there and she nosey ass fuck."

"Girl? You got a girl? So why did you come here?"

I was completely taken off guard.

"Yeah something like that and when I see something I want I go for it. You got a problem with that?" He asked.

"No," I responded quickly.

If he didn't care about his woman neither should I. Nothing was going to get in the way of me and him. At least not tonight.

"Yeah so let me see if you about that little cute note you wrote," he smirked.

This man was so fucking fine. I went to where he was at and grabbed my cup downing my drink. I got on my knees unbuckling his belt. He smelled so fucking good. I knew my panties was already drenched. I was hoping he was packing because I would be truly disappointed. He was too fine to be slacking. I didn't have to hope for long because his dick was so hard, I knew he was working with something. I grabbed it out of his draws and massaged it with my hand. It was so pretty and long and even had a curve. He was smoking his blunt and looking down at me.

"Go head," He nodded.

I put the head in my mouth and sucked on it slowly while massaging the shaft. His dick even tasted good too. I bet he never had nobody deep throat his dick before, at least not like I can. I was going to show him just what the fuck I can do. Looking up at him he had his eyes closed and was biting on his bottom lip. I put his dick further in my mouth inch by inch while massaging his balls. He grabbed my head while fucking my mouth. It was a lot to deal with because he had a long dick, but I wasn't backing out now. I sucked harder and harder. I felt his dick throbbing in my mouth, so I knew he was about to cum and I was going to swallow every fucking drop.

"Shit, Hypnotic I'm about to cum," he said right on que.

Spit was dripping all down my mouth. You would've thought I was super head in this bitch.

I heard him groaning as he shot a load down my throat.

"Damn girl," he said out of breath.

I knew I had his ass now.

"Bitch you lyinggggg!" Mia screamed.

"No bitch I'm serious," I laughed.

It was Sunday so we were out having brunch. These unlimited mimosas had us lit already. I was still high off the dick. Trey's dick. It's been two days and I couldn't stop fantasizing or thinking about it. I had to wait until I was in person with Mia to see the look on her face. I knew she was just as excited as me.

"It was so big and even had a curveeee," I said.

"Oh my god I love a curveeee," she laughed.

"Have you talked to him since?" She asked.

"Yeah, I did, we text here and there. He's a busy man so he doesn't be on his phone a lot. We are supposed to be meeting up soon so that's a good thing. Whenever he can get away from his girlfriend," I said.

"Girlfriend?" Mia asked.

"Yeah but they're on the verge of breaking up so I'm not even sweating it."

"Men are liars. They always use that excuse," Mia said.

"Well he doesn't take me as a liar, and I believe him."

I ended that real quick. Won't plant any negative seeds on my future baby daddy.

"Okay girl I'm just saying. Be safe, that's all, "she said.

The waitress came back and filled up our mimosas. Talking about Trey I just received a text from him.

TREY: *I seen what that mouth felt like, when I'm going to see what that pussy feels like?*

ME: *Whenever you want to.*

TREY: *That's what I like to hear. When I call you later to come downstairs, come downstairs.*

ME: *How do you know where I live?*

TREY: *I got my ways. You know who I am baby.*

I don't even know why I questioned that. One thing I knew for sure was when he told me to come downstairs, my ass was coming running.

Yasmine

"Yes Jay?" I answered my phone.

"When can I see you?" He asked me.

"I just been so busy I'll let you know."

"You used to have so much time for me before," he responded.

Yeah because you weren't so damn annoying, I thought rolling my eyes.

"I'm going to call you back," I said hanging up not even giving him a chance to respond.

This man was like a thorn in my back. In the beginning he wasn't so bad. Then, he started catching feelings and shit making me uncomfortable. I told him from the jump I wasn't into all of that. I didn't have time for any of that. He was one of my main customers at the club. He would come every two weeks and request me to dance for him and give me money to pay off the next few months of my bills, so I wasn't complaining at all. He then started to ask me to come out with him places and so on. I wasn't with it in the beginning, but then he said he was going to pay me for it. Why the fuck not? He started to pay me to go out with him and flaunt me around his friends. Whatever made him sleep better at night. If I was getting paid for it, it was the least of my worries. Yeah, we had sex here and there. I'm a female with needs okay. He might have been a little weird, but I can always get around that. Randomly out the blue he started to tell me that he loves me and sending bouquets of flowers to my home. I asked him, why? His response was that he wanted to treat me good. This shit was getting too out of hand.

JAY: *I love you.*

See what I mean? I was going to have to tell him about himself and sooner than I thought.

I just finished doing my set on stage and that shit had me drained. What started as just a little here and there gig for me became a full-time career. I told myself I was only going to just do this for a while but years later I'm still here. Making more money than I ever made in my life. Shaking my ass was treating me well. After counting my money with my home girl Bubbles, we went to the bar to relax and get a drink.

"Rocsi let me get a margarita," I told the bartender.

"You killed it tonight Bambi," Bubbles said.

Bambi was my stage name here. Complimenting my long sexy legs of course.

"Don't I always?"

I was joking but we both knew it was true. I was basically the one, if not the only main attraction at the club. Bubbles wasn't bad looking but her body took up for the looks that she lacked. She was cool so she was like the only girl I really fucked with in here. You can't trust these stripper bitches. She was on a little high right now. A lot of the girls here did drugs to get them relaxed, but a few shots of tequila did the trick for me. I wasn't into all that other stuff.

"Isn't that Jay?" She asked me.

I turned around and low and behold it was. I was hoping he didn't start any shit here tonight because I wasn't in the mood for his bullshit. He wasn't even a bad looking dude he just did too much at times. He reminded me of how Mekhi Phifer looked in Paid in Full, fine as hell! He always kept himself put together well. That was what attracted me to him in the first place. I loved a chocolate man.

I saw the bottle girls coming to his section, with some strippers behind them. One of the strippers, Cinnamon went to Jay and started dancing on him like her life depended on it. If looks could kill I would be dead because Jay was burning a hole in me.

"You want to go over there and stop that shit?" Bubbles asked me.

He was basically trying to make a fool of me. Everybody knew how we were or was. I didn't give a fuck though. Maybe he would start blowing their phones up and leave me the fuck alone.

"Girl hell no! I'm good!" I laughed.

A few minutes after when he saw I wasn't paying him any attention. He pushed cinnamon off him and walked towards me.

"So, you didn't see me over there?" He asked me.

"Yes, I saw you Jay," I replied.

"So why you didn't come over there and speak?" He asked me.

"Because you seem to be having a good time."

"Yasmine don't fucking play with me."

He grabbed my wrist like he wanted to break it.

Yeah, my night was ending early, this man gets crazier as the days go by. I fucked up giving him this pussy.

"I have to use the bathroom, I'm going to come to your section in a little baby," I lied to him.

Seeming satisfied he let me go and walked away.

"You really going over there?" Bubbles asked me.

"Like hell I'm not! I'm going home girl! See you later!" I laughed and walked towards the locker room to get my things and be on my way.

I went through the back of the club and thought I saw Trey Red Benz go by, but maybe my eyes were playing tricks on me. I got in my car and took my ass home. The way Jay was always acting I think I soon needed to walk with protection on me.

Sasha

TREY: *Come outside.*

ME: *I just can't leave in the middle of work.*

TREY: *I didn't ask you that.*

I went to the locker room to start to get my things packed, I guess my night was ending early.

"Excuse me."

I heard somebody yell as I felt my shoulder get pushed.

"You're fucking excused!" I yelled back.

I saw Bambi frown her nose up at me, bitch thought she was all that. I couldn't stand her ass. She looked like she wanted to say something but also looked as if she was in a rush, so she just finished walking.

Getting in front of the club I saw Trey pull up, so I got in his car.

"You just missed your friend," laughed.

"Who?" He asked.

"Yasmine, Bambi, whatever y'all call that bitch."

"Don't start your shit."

I put on my seat belt and crossed my arms.

"You still mad at me?" He asked me.

"I could never be mad, you're not my man," I replied.

"It wasn't like that, she asked me to just drop her off at the mall and I had to pick up something too," he responded.

"Ummm hmm."

Earlier this week imagine my surprise when I saw Trey and I'm guessing his girlfriend or, supposedly ex-girlfriend at the mall. Mia wanted to go up to them and say something, but I was honestly hurt. In the little bit of time I've been dealing with Trey we spent almost every day together, so I really don't know how they were still together. Either she was dumb or knew he was out doing him. It had to be something. He told me they relationship was over but from the looks of it, it was hard to fucking tell what the hell was going on. I was ignoring his calls and texts all week.

"I don't have any reason to lie to you," he said.
"I'm sure you don't" I replied.
"You don't miss me?" He asked me.
I started to blush. Of course, I missed him.
"A little," I lied.
I was obsessed with him. I noticed we was getting on the highway. I thought we were going to my place like we usually do.
"Where are we going?" I asked him.
"I got to go drop something off," he responded turning up the music. He always did that when he didn't want to talk anymore. At first, I thought it was rude, but now I was getting used to it. We ended up in front of some house. I don't even know where we were. He answered the phone and told someone a girl was going to drop the bag off. A girl? What girl?

"You see that first house on the right? When you see the light turn off and back on go in the trunk and grab the black duffel bag. Knock on the door two times and then knock one more time. The guy is going to hand you a bag and then walk away. I'm going around the block and I'm going to meet you on the corner."

He basically told me without asking.

"What?!"

"Pay the fuck attention. Do as I say," he responded.

Right after he said that I saw the light turn off and back on, so I did as I was told. Some guy opened the door and before I could even get a good look at his face, he grabbed the bag from me quickly and switched it with another bag that looked completely identical. I walked from in front of the house and walked towards the corner. Trey was nowhere to be found. I left my bag in the car, so I didn't have a phone on me to call him. Here I was in the middle of nowhere with a bag full of who the fuck knows. I started sweating and panicking because it now felt like five minutes went pass. I started to walk because being on this corner was no help. As soon as I walked across the street a car with its light on damn near blinded me.

"Get your stupid ass in the car, where the fuck you are going?!" I heard Trey yell.

I quickly got in the car and sat the bag in the back seat.

"Why did you take so long?" I asked him.

"I had to make sure nobody was following me," He replied.

Finally, after a long drive back we got in front of my house and he took the bag from the back seat. He unzipped the bag and it was bundles of money. I couldn't even guess how much it was. He took three bundles out and threw them on my lap.

"It's more where that came from," He said.

"What's that supposed to mean?" I asked him.

He gave me a few stacks here and there, but it was nothing compared to this.

"Fuck with me you'll see," he responded and gave me a kiss.

"You not coming up?" I asked him.

"Nah I have to go handle something, but I'll see you in a little. If not, then tomorrow," he responded.

"Okay baby."

We said goodbye and as soon as I got inside, I ran to my room to count the money.

"Ten thousand dollars just to drop a bag off?!" I yelled to myself. Hell yeah! I wouldn't have to work in the club for too long now.

Candace

March 2018

As I was lying in bed watching Nas put some cologne on, I still felt like I was floating on the clouds. We just had a morning session and I swear I didn't know how he had so much energy right now. I had a red satin sheet wrapped around me as I was sprawled out across the bed.

"Babe I'm about to go to the club. Call me before you leave to go to the mall. Love you," he said as grabbed my ass and kissed me.

He was opening a new club and on the first night I was just going to have my birthday party. Killing two birds with one stone and celebrating for both occasions.

"Matter fact call me when you find the dress you are wearing because it seems like you need some supervision when you go shopping," He said.

He always complained about what I brought to wear but always loved it and wind up fucking me right out of it. So, he says all that now, but I know what he means.

"Baby what you mean? Stop being dramatic. I promise it's not going to be anything crazy," I replied.

"Keep playing with me Candy you gone see."

He just was talking to talk. I had him all the way wrapped around my finger. On the low he had me too.

Two hours later I was up and ready. Just before I was getting ready to leave, I grabbed my vitamins container for biotin and took my birth control pill. Ever since I got with Nas he's been trying to get me pregnant, so I had to keep refilling my prescription. I know I know. Loving and Wealthy man? Why am I doing this behind his back? I already told him when I was with my ex Deuce, I had a miscarriage, but I didn't tell him it was a few. I know I shouldn't even be thinking that's going to happen again before it even happens, but I just can't shake the thought and I'm just not prepared right now if it does happen. I don't think I can even phantom another miscarriage. One day I will stop taking them but just not today. Interrupting my thoughts, I heard my phone ring.

"Hello?" I spoke into the phone.

"What time you going to be ready?" Emerald asked.

"I'm about to leave out now. Why?" I asked.

"Trey getting on my nerves thinking I'm going to see a guy."

"You? Going to see a guy? He needs to get over himself. Better yet you need to get over him," I said.

"Candy don't start."

She knew how I felt about him too, so I had no filter when it came to Trey. She deserves so much better. I hated him and I don't know why she still waste her time. Yes, I know it's because of me kind of that they got together. I'm the one who told him we were coming to the Barbecue, but after all the bullshit he put her through mentally not even physically it's now up to her to move on. Everyone has their own timing to see things the outside does see so I just pray in due time she will wake up.

Emerald

Candy better had been glad I love her because she told me come with her to get one thing. We been in this damn mall for about four hours. We were out looking for an outfit for her birthday party she was having at another club Nas was opening. Trey was bugging me thinking I was out doing who knows what. He was always down my back about the simplest shit. I told him I was with Candy, sent him pictures and all. Guess what? I'm still lying. In his head me and Candy planned the whole shit all out.

"Em! How does this look on me? I think this is the one."

My best friend Candy asked me as she walked out the dressing room with a nice short red leather dress with the sides see through. Yeah, the dress was fly as hell, but I knew Nas wasn't having that.

"Let me call my YOUR man and see what he thinks."

I grabbed my phone out of my bag to act like I was calling him. Candy grabbed my phone out my hand and sucked her teeth.

"I'm grown girl please! Seriously, how does it look on me? I love it," Candy said as she looked in the mirror and smoothed the dress out. The dress went nice with her chocolate complexion. My best friend was the shit. Never the one to hate on another female. Candy was about 5'6 with what you call an hourglass shape. Some people thought she went under the knife but no she was all natural. Her ass was always testing Nas and having him go crazy over the shit she wore. She had a black bob with a middle part and slanted eyes. She was a brown skin beauty.

"Yes Candy, this dress is the one. Just don't be calling me when Nas tear that shit apart."

"Girl don't worry about Nas, I could handle him," Candy said while sticking her tongue out. *Nasty ass.*

We waited on the line to pay for her things and then left. We got into my black Mercedes-Benz SUV that Trey brought me for my 25th birthday. Being that I was the ride, I dropped Candy off.

Finally arriving home, I sat in my car mentally preparing myself for all his bitching he was going to do. Don't get me wrong, Trey wasn't always like this. Just over the time he gotten so insecure. Always thought I was out doing something. Walking towards the door I opened it with my key. Trey was sitting on the couch playing his game. I dropped my bag on the counter and just stared at him. A lot of guys didn't have waves anymore, but my baby always had his looking just right. He was still as handsome as the first day I laid eyes on him. It just was his attitude that made him ugly.

"You had a good time with your nigga on yall date?" He asked me as he walked towards the kitchen.

Here we go, I thought. I poured me a glass of Wine just to calm my nerves.

"Trey you know I was with Candy."

"Fuck that hoe, you think somebody dumb. Yeah alright! I got something for your ass."

"And what the fuck is that supposed to mean?"

"You'll find out," he said as he went to sit back on the couch and play his game. Now I was getting fed up because what the fuck was that really supposed to mean? I stood in front of the TV.

Fuck his game!

"Hello! What is that supposed to mean?" I yelled at him.

"Just what the fuck it sounds like Em. You aren't going to be playing me like I'm some basic ass nigga."

Trying to be patient with his ass I counted from five backwards to one.

Woosahh.

"Trey I told you I was at the mall okay," I said as I sat down next to him.

"So, let me see your phone then if you don't got shit to hide," he said as he looked me in my eyes. I passed him my phone and watched him go through my call log, messages, and my social media inboxes... Why the hell did he have to do all of this after I told him what it was? Why couldn't he just believe me? Seeming satisfied he passed me my phone back. After a few minutes of silence, he finally spoke.

"Baby, I'm sorry for tripping, it just that I love you so much and don't want you to leave me. Lately, I been feeling like you tired of a nigga and want to move on," He apologetically told me.

"Leave you? Why would I want to leave you baby?! I love you. You know that."

"You love me? So, come closer and come give me a kiss."

I moved closer to him and gave him a peck on his lips.

"Damn, that's all I get?" He asked rubbing my leg. I got on top of him and wrapped my arms around the back of his head while I kissed him passionately... He was a kisser, so I knew I was turning him on. He grabbed my ass with both of his hands. He started kissing my neck as I held my eyes close just enjoying it. He was starting to make me feel so good. Reversed roles on me real fast.

"You love daddy, right? Tell me you love me."

"I love you daddy," I moaned.

Yeah, he had me now. I'm pretty sure he knew it too. Just that fast, I forgot I was even mad at him. He didn't even have to rotate my hips anymore; I was grinding on him myself. Grabbing my shirt and taking it off he then grabbed my right breast and started to lick on it gently. I started to feel him harden under me. I felt like I was on the urge of Cumming just from him sucking on my breast. Grabbing my legs with now my left breast in his mouth he changed positions with me and now I was under him and he was on top of me. Once he stopped sucking on my breast, he started to kiss my stomach. Being that I had on a skirt he just moved my red thong to the side and started to suck on my clit while he rubbed my breast with his thumb and index finger. I felt my essence running from my pussy to the crack of my ass. Trey was enjoying it because he started moaning just as much as me. He looked in my eyes as I grabbed the back of his head and put two of his fingers in my pussy slowly moving them in and out. He knew doing that was going to make me cum. It always did, and the way he was moaning while devouring me wasn't making it any better.

– "Cum for daddy," he told me as he started to move his fingers with a faster pace. My stomach felt like it was doing back flips as I released all over his face. He stood up and started kissing me again as I tasted my own juices. Grabbing his dick, he entered me. Adjusting to his size, he started pumping in and out as I sucked on his bottom lip. He grabbed my ass so he could get deeper in my pussy.

"Take this dick! I'm going to get it right baby I promise," he said as he started going harder and harder. I couldn't even get anything out even if I tried. My pussy started to tighten on his dick as I felt his dick throbbing as he pulled out and came on my stomach.

I woke up the next morning and noticed Trey was gone. I called his phone more than enough times but still got his voicemail. *Maybe something came up,* I thought. I got out the bed to use the bathroom and saw a stack of money and a note that read *"Had to handle something with Maine didn't want to wake you, love you babe. I'm sorry again"*. He always thought money was going to fix our problems when it was the disrespect that was the problem, but whatever. Not having any time to dwell on this. I started to get ready and start my day.

After I got out the shower, I grabbed my favorite vanilla scented lotion putting it onto my body. Standing in front of the mirror, admiring my frame. Yeah, I'm not as small as I was once was, but I think my curves filled out nice. I walked into my walk-in closet looking for something to wear today... I decided on a white crop top sweater, denim jean jumper with my Red Manning Cartel leather heels. Grabbing my Red Chanel bag, I sprayed some perfume on me and went out the door. On my way to the shop, I did my normal stop and got me some breakfast from Secrets. This was the best Diner in town, I swear. After I got my food I headed to the shop. Opening the door and greeting everybody. It was very busy on Fridays, so I sometimes came to help. I used to be a stylist, but I started going into a different career path.

Candy wanted to make this a one stop shop so they literally did everything here. Weaves, blowouts, dreads, nails, eyebrows. When I say everything, I mean everything. Dreads were mainly what I did here and braids. I used to have them myself but decided I wanted to try something new and it's been two years now. Candy always kept my shit looking fly. She recently colored it milk chocolate and added some blonde highlights.

Candy was on the phone blushing, so I knew she had to be talking to Nas. I bet she was buttering him all up until he saw what she was going to wear tonight to the club.

"Okay, babe I love you too. Be safe," Candy smiled into the phone while hanging it up.

"Emmmyyyyy!" Candy smiled and looked at me.

I knew she wanted something because that's the only time she calls me by my nickname she gave me.

"What you want now Candace?" I sternly asked.

"Okay, so I know this is last minute buttttt, Nas cousin is coming out here to handle business with Nas and you know how you're the best dread stylist around andddddd-"

"Really Candy?!" I asked cutting her off.

"I know, I know, I know, Nas said that he's going to look out so it's nothing to worry about. You know he got you sis. Please, because I already said yes," she mumbled at the end.

"Of course, you did. Better be glad I love my brother. What time they supposed to be coming? You know dreads take forever so I hope not long!"

"Soon, he just went to get him from the airport".

"Okay. Em, Nas just told me they're coming around the corner now. He wanted to make sure nobody else was in the chair," Candy said.

The nerve of him, I thought.

The front door of the salon opened and Nas walked in. Candy was all smiles.

"Nas, so where your little cousin at? I'm ready to get this over with. Just know, you owe me big time."

"Little? I don't know what the hell Candy told you, but my cousin is a grown ass man ma."

Right after Nas said that that I swear a Chocolate Greek God walked inside the salon. Okay, when Candy told me it was Nas cousin I automatically thought it was a little cousin coming into town wanting to party for Candy birthday and the club opening and needed his hair done. But, not this fine creature. I know I have a "man" at home and not supposed to be thinking like this buttttt damn! I'm only human, right? I looked at Candy and she looked at me smiling. She knew what she was doing. She hated Trey.

"Aight, well I'm about to get my dreads twisted so imma holla at you," The Chocolate Greek God, oops I mean Nas cousin said into his phone.

"Sorry didn't mean to be rude. Good afternoon ladies. Now who is the one that took the time out their day to make sure my head is straight, so I can thank you personally?"

He smiled looking back from me to Yasmine. Oh, lawdddd I had to squeeze my legs together because damn he had me! He was tall too just like Nas maybe a little taller at 6'2 or 6'3. He had dreads that went to the middle of his back and black piercing eyes. Or so I thought. He had on some black timbs with black jeans and a white shirt that matched his white teeth with a black leather jacket.

"Not I! I can't be next to your family for too long," Yasmine said.

"Huh?" he asked confused.

"She and Yasir got a little beef. You know how he is," Nasir said.

Yasir was Nas twin brother and him and Yasmine hated one another. I don't even know how that came into play, but they cannot be in a room for too long together. He's always mentioning her stripping and Yasmine always mentioning him being a "bitch ass nigga" so we always try to keep them two apart.

"It's not little beef. He's a bitch ass...".

"Yeah, Emmy tell him it's you so he could thank you! Personallyyy," Candy said cutting Yasmine off and dragging personally!

See I knew she was behind this mess! He started walking towards me as my heart started racing. You know when you feel that magnetic feeling with somebody? Or lust? Who knows at this moment? Like the vibe just be so strong. That's exactly what I felt right now. Get it together girl, I thought.

"So, I'm guessing it's you Emmy? Emmy short for what?" He asked me with his hand out to shake my hand.

"Emerald and you?" I asked as I shook his hand.

"Vito."

I felt a shock go through my body. I swear I wasn't being dramatic right now.

"Emerald? My favorite color is green you know. I might have to keep you around. Depending on how you hook me up," he winked at me. I felt like I fainted, but I was still standing. Is that even possible?

"Oh really. We just going to have to see," I said to him. Damn! When you flirt but don't intentionally mean to flirt. Shit.

"Candy, come with me to your office really quick so you could help me get the pins for the dreads?"

"I have some by my station. Let me see— "

Cutting her off, "CANDY! It's fine, I like the ones in the office better. Just come. She knew what she was doing, and she knew why I wanted her to come to the office. We walked into her office and I started firing off questions back to back.

"You knew he was that fine right? Why did you tell me it was just a cousin and not a damn god? Why you set me up? How do I look?"

"I haven't seen him in a long time, so what I can say is that he did get a little more muscle. Girl, nobody set you up, I didn't know you was going to get all woozy. At least not that quick. And you look fine baby like you always do. SOOO what do you think?" She smiled at me.

"You know I'm with Trey."

"FUCK HIS ASS!" She yelled. I knew that was going to be her response. They hated each other.

"Yeah whatever Candy," I said as I went to the mirror to make sure everything was still intact

"Damn, cuz got you like that already? Hee-hee," her silly ass had the nerve to say.

"Well, help me get the wax and pins so I can really make it seem like that's what we came back here for," I said.

Grabbing my things, we went back out. Yasmine was getting ready to leave and Candy was already done for the day.

Being that it was the party tonight she made it known she was closing the shop early. I started to proceed with Vito's hair. Grabbing the cape, I put it around his neck and told him let's go to the sink so I can wash his hair. His dreads didn't really look bad at all. You can tell he kept up with himself. Not that it mattered to me, just saying. We talked while I washed his hair and all I could do was stare at his eyes while they were closed. He had some long pretty eyelashes. I don't know how I didn't notice that when he first walked in. He opened his eyes and caught me staring at him. Shit! He just laughed and closed them back.

I towel dried his hair while bringing him to the dryer so his hair can dry a little before I start the twisting. It was now almost five-thirty. Yasmine left and now Nas and Candy were getting up to leave. Leave? So, she was going to leave me here by myself with Vito? What the hell.

"I thought you guys were staying?" I asked.

"Yeah, but Nas is hungry so we're going to get something to eat first before we get ready. See y'all later at the party. Vito don't forget to thank Em like you said. Personallyyyyy," she laughed while walking to the door.

"Mind your business," Nas told her as he slapped her on the ass. I went to the doors and locked it because nobody else was coming to get any more services done.

"Okay let's knock this out really quick," I told Vito.

About 2 ½ hours later I was finally done. We talked and got to know each other during that time. He was a real cool dude. Not just because he was fine. I like that he could hold a conversation and have something to talk about. I turned the chair around so he can see my work. He kept talking shit the whole time saying I better hook him up and probably lost my touch because I do more real estate now. I knew I was going to get the last laugh. He looked in the mirror with nothing more to say. Yeah, I knew he liked them because he had no reason not to.

"Shit Em. You really did your thing. I'm feeling this ma. Real talk. Thank you," He said to me as he went in his pocket. Handing me money to pay me, I noticed it was entirely too much.

"Vito, I don't charge that much it's fine," I said handling him back some hundreds, yes hundreds.

"It's not just that. You canceled the rest of your day just to make sure I was good. I really appreciate that. And you hooked my shit up. Think of it as a tip," he said. Fine, I wasn't going to fight anybody down to return any money.

"Well, let's get going I got a few things to handle before this party," I said to him as we walked to the door after I turned the lights off in the shop.

He grabbed my hand and pulled me close to him. Um what was going on? It was dark so I couldn't really see him that much because the sun was already gone, but I could smell him. He smelled so good. He hugged me and whispered in my ear "Thank you". His lips touched my ear when he said hugging me tighter.

"Mhmmmm."

Wait did I just moan from a hug? I immediately started coughing to try and play it off like something was caught in my throat.

He started laughing, "Damn Em what was that? You good?"

He knew what he was doing to me. I was so embarrassed.

"Uhhhhh I don't know. But see you tonight get home safe," I told him as I rushed us both outside the salon and locked up. Rushing to my car only thing I was thinking was, *got damn!*

Trey

    I hope when I get in Em don't be blowing me up with questions asking where I been. I don't know what it was, but shit just changed with us. I think it was because she wasn't on my back as much as she was before. Some people call it insecure some people call it controlling but I don't give a fuck. It's wasn't any of that. Just little shit like that be causing niggas to stray. Yeah, I love her but; I don't know shit was just different now. I feel like I'm not the same nigga I once was before. I was getting more money because I got a new connect now so I was doing well. With Emerald, she wanted that good guy type shit. She knew that wasn't me, so I don't understand why she always tried to force it on me. Now, Sasha? She was all for it. Never tried to get in my head or tried to change me. She accepted me for who I was and that's why I fucked with her.

"Babe, you going to that bitch Candy party tonight because I'm going. You are coming with me?" Sasha asked me, better known as hypnotic.

Damn she was so smart until she was dumb.

"How the fuck I'm going to go with you to a party my girl going to be at?"

She rolled her eyes. Oh boy! Not this shit again.

"Girl? Wow Trey. I thought we were done with that, I guess not."

"You know what it is so stop playing. Just let it flow baby girl you know daddy love you. I told you I keep my stuff there. I wouldn't want you involved in any of that."

I lied. I told her I kept some drugs and shit stashed at Emerald crib. She asked me why I didn't take it out or even bring it to her crib. I made up so lame story about how I cared about her safety and didn't want her involved in any of that. She rolled her eyes again, but I knew my baby and knew what she wanted.

"I'm just saying, you always talk about how she not me or make you feel how I make you feel. So, you really love me? Let me know what's up because if you still want to play these games. I can do me."

She knew I hated when she talked like that. Grabbing her by her neck I told her, "I didn't hear what the fuck you said. Run that by me again. You are going to do what?"

I grabbed her neck a little harder because I knew she wasn't going to be able to get her words out.

"Oh, that's what I thought. Stop that fucking crying and come give daddy a kiss."

I knew what I can and cannot do with Sasha. Deep down I feel like she liked this fighting shit. She just got on my damn nerves with all that nagging. I like to move on my own time and nobody else's. Don't get me wrong Sasha was my bitch. She was sexy as fuck too. About 5'6 with some nice long legs. I loved when the shits were on my shoulders. She was getting a little thick on me too. In a good way and I was loving that shit. Yeah, I know it sound dumb trying to fuck with a bitch that sucked my dick on the first night, but she was something new and exciting. Put it this way, she was going to suck my dick regardless. We were rocking with each other ever since. Lost in my thoughts I felt my dick in Sasha mouth. She knew exactly what the fuck I liked. She was looking at me with her piercing eyes while she made a mess on my dick while stroking it.

"Damnnn baby, suck that dick. You love me baby?"

She nodded yes.

"So, make this dick cum. Let me give you something to taste in your mouth."

She started moaning. The sight was just turning me the fuck on. Sasha got off on sucking my dick too. My baby loved that shit. She started to suck faster and harder. I grabbed the back of her head as I released in her mouth and she swallowed every bit of it.

My phone started ringing and I knew it was Emerald. I told Sasha be quite as she sat on my lap.

"So, this is what we do now?!" She yelled into the phone.

I knew she was going to be on that shit.

"I told you babe I got caught up with Maine. My phone died and the nigga had to drive all the way to Jersey babe. We just are getting back. I'm going to see you in like thirty minutes," I said as I hung up.

Damn she was annoying.

"Oh, so I'm Maine now?" Sasha asked me.

"Turn that ass around let me get some of that before I dip."

I changed the subject as I pulled the condom out my pocket and put it on. I slide my dick in Sasha and I bet she shut that shit the fuck up.

Vito

It's my cousin girl birthday party at our new club opening tonight. Nas and I are partners with our club businesses and our shit is booming. This was the best decision that I've made yet. I stopped being in the streets first because it either ends up two ways, in a body bag or behind bars for a long ass time. Nas was hesitant and hardheaded at first but he finally jumped on board. I don't really like to be all in the mix and shit but I got love for my cousin so I was going to come out to party not just as a boss, and with Emerald coming that gave me another reason to come along, just to see what shawty was about. No lie she had me a little interested... Right now, I was in my hotel room waiting for Nas and Candy to come and get me so we could get moving. They let me know I was welcomed to stay with them, but I didn't want to invade their privacy and shit. For now, it was just pleasure but I made it known to Nas I came out here on a business trip. I'm originally from New York but I moved out to Cali to get more money. I held Cali down and Nas held New York down.

"Babe how long you are going to be there? I miss you already," Chantel told me.

She was some chick I fucked with down in Cali. Yeah, I had love for her, but I couldn't see me making her wifey. She did have some good pussy though.

"I told you I won't be here for too long. I'm not going to talk too much but you'll see me soon. I'm going to hit you back later though Nas on the other line."

"Yooooo," I answered.

"Yeah come downstairs we here!" he yelled into the phone.

Nigga sounded like he was at the party already. Candy brings the life outta that man. That's why I fuck with her. If my cousin was happy, I'm good. I grabbed my piece and made my way out the door. I wasn't going anywhere without my shit, especially around these grimy ass New York niggas. I got to the first floor and saw the lady behind the desk watching me hard, she was alright. Something I could fuck with while I'm down here. She better stop playing before I throw this dick all in her.

"Vitoooooo over here!" I heard Candy yell out.

Her body was damn near hanging out the car window. How the fuck we going to a party and they look like they just left a damn party? I walked to my cousin Benz and got in. I gave him a dap and Candy a hug. First thing that was going through my mind was why the hell do she got this shit on? I looked at Candy, then at Nas. He knew what the fuck I was thinking and just shrugged his shoulders. Yeah that nigga was pussy whip.

"So, what do you think about Em?" Candy asked as soon as I saw down.

"I mean she's aightttttt," I said.

"Yeah, okay. Well she is coming with her bum ass nigga so don't be on your best behavior," she winked.

"Candy stop starting your shit. Let that man be!" Nas said.

"I'm just saying don't let him get in your way," she laughed.

"If she got a man obviously, she is satisfied with what she got. I didn't come out here for all that. I'm good," I told her. *Over here trying to play matchmaker and shit.*

"Well I'm just saying but whatever. Oh Nas! Turn this up you know this my shit!" She yelled. He turned the radio up and Cardi B Bodak Yellow playing. He had the nerve to be singing this shit too. They were made for one another.

Sasha

Trey had another thing coming if he thought I'm going be home alone while he goes party with that bitch trying to look like the couple of the year. He doesn't even want her ass! Talking about some he got to give it time because he doesn't really want to hurt her. Fuck all that shit! What about me? What I do know is that I'm going to that party tonight too!

"Come over here and zip my dress up for me," I told to Mia.

"Girl, you can barely fit the shit anymore and why are we going to this party anyway. Are you trying to hurt yourself even more?" She asked rolling her eyes and zipping up my dress. She wasn't really a big fan of Trey and I really didn't give a fuck because she wasn't the one fucking him. I was!

"We're going because I am in a party mood!" She asks too many damn questions.

"Who in the world cares to party while they're pregnant."

Yeah, I was pregnant, and Trey didn't know. I didn't want to tell him too soon because I know kids is not his thing right now. One way or another I was going to have him to myself and this right here was the token. I was barely showing at all. You wouldn't even think I was pregnant. I was almost five months pregnant. I thought something was wrong because I was barely showing but the doctor told me everything was fine. Trey is so dumb he didn't even notice the signs. I used to have a hell of morning sicknesses and everything. Yes, I trapped him, so what. He made sure to strap up every time with us but that don't mean a few holes in a condom wouldn't do the trick. After a few tries tadah, baby on board! I knew he would leave Emerald ass now.

"Us! Now come on let's go," I told Mia.

Of course, Trey didn't know but, he was about to get the surprise of his life. Let's see if all that talk about how he can't stand to be around her, and all is true or not.

This club was nice! I told Trey he should've got on board with Nas, but he said this wasn't for him so whatever.

If he was still paid that's all I cared about. Just like the other club BLACKOUT I, we were at BLACKOUT II. They basically had the same outline. I went to the first BLACKOUT a few times so that's how I was aware of the similarities. Mia and I went to the bar to order drinks. I was just getting a glass of wine to calm my nerves because I knew like hell when Trey sees me, it wasn't going to be pretty. Nor did I fucking care to make it pretty. I'm tired of him playing games with me and with a baby on the way he needs to get it together. Mia got her an apple martini. That was her all-time favorite drink. I knew my friend was annoyed with me but being the good friend, she was. She's right here by my side.

"For all y'all that's here enjoying yourselves. It's because of these men right here. So, show some respect," The DJ said.

I saw Nas with Candy and a guy I never saw before. He was fine as hell too, with dreads. I wonder why I never seen him before. The light went to their section and in the far back I saw Trey next to Emerald. I swear steam was coming from my ears. This is the second time I ever saw them together. He didn't look like he was annoyed sitting there as much as she "annoys" him like he says she do.

"Come on Mia. Let the night begin," I told her and got closer to their sections.

I grabbed the first guy I saw and started dancing on him. Which was perfect timing too because the DJ started playing just the right song. "Sex with me" by Rihanna. I took the rest of my wine back and started working my shit like we were fucking but just with clothes on.

Sex with me, so amazing
All this all work, no vacation
Stay up off my Instagram with your temptation
Hit a switch on a fake nigga like a station
Sex with me, so amazing
Sex with me, so amazing
Vodka and water, and a lemon
And a few other things I cannot mention

I was dancing like this was my man and we was making love on the dance floor. Since Trey wanted to play so was I. The guy wasn't bad looking, but he didn't look as good as Trey do. I saw Mia through the side of my eyes edging me on. I looked up at the section Trey was in and low and behold his eyes were burning holes right through me. I laughed and turned around and got on top of the guy who now, had a hard ass dick. I knew he was confused to why he got so lucky tonight. I started grinding on top of him.

Ooh nana nana five fingers on it
Five fingers, hit it like you want it
I'ma hit it like I'm on it
Straight shots of the Buddha
Shots, shots, shots, shots

Baby, I'ma pick your poison
Ooh-we, oh-yeah (hmm na na na)
You gon' need it
I'm off that la-la
I'ma get it real like the Jacuzzi, (ah yeah)

    Everybody eyes were on me. I had almost the whole club attention. I knew what I was doing being that I use to be a dancer before Trey came into my life and told me after a few months he didn't want me dancing which I happily obliged to because doing runs with him was far better than the club. I felt I didn't even need to strip anyway. What I was making was double of what I made in the club. If my bills stayed paid and my pockets stay fat, I had no worries at all.

    Just like that I got up and walked toward the front door of the club. My night was done. Two can play that game. My phone indicated I got a text message.

TREY: *Dumb bitch!*

Ha-ha! Now my night was done!

Emerald

I'm starting to think it was a bad idea coming here. Trey and I was good at first but the next thing you know out the blue his mood had changed. Every time he says he's going to change it just go back to him being a dick! Never fails!

"Yo, you ready? I got shit to do?" He asked me. We weren't even here for fucking long. No, I wasn't ready it's my best friend party.

"No Trey if you want to you can leave," I told him, hoping by me saying it so sadly it would change his mind and make him feel bad.

"Aight, imma holla at you," He said and walked away.

What? That's it? I'm tired of this shit. I don't know why I just won't leave him alone. Every time I do, I just get so lonely and I'm so comfortable with being with him it's just something I'm used to. I walked back to the section and everybody was drunk and having the time of their lives. Candace and Nas was practically fucking looking all drunk and in love. I don't envy what they have but sometimes I just don't understand how Nas and Trey are two completely different people. I'm happy for her though, she lucked up with Nas for sure. She was grinding on him and he was rubbing her ass with not just one hand, both of his hands while they kissed. It was getting awkward just staring at them but sometimes I can't believe how Candy had Nas ass all open. More power to her. I turned to my left and saw Vito sitting down with a bottle of Ace of Spades drinking it. He motioned for me to come over to him. I looked both ways to make sure Trey wasn't around. But, then again why should I care?

– "Why you are sitting over there all alone looking all sad?" He asked me. I was smiling so hard forgetting I was even sad. He was just so beautifully created.

"I'm not sad just a little tired," I said and fake yawned.

"Oh okay. You look nice. I don't know about all that you had on earlier," he laughed.

He knew he was lying because I looked good earlier and I damn sure look good tonight. My own "man" didn't even tell me I looked good come to think about it. I had on a black body fitting dress with some leather red shoe boots that Came up to my thigh. My red lipstick went perfect with my shoes too.

"What's wrong with what I had on earlier?" I questioned.

He looked me up and down and licked his lips.

"Nothing was wrong I was just playing, you're beautiful. Don't be afraid to shows it off," he said.

"I'm not afraid to show it off," I said sitting down next to him.

"I wouldn't be afraid to show you off," he said. I jerked my neck in his direction to make sure I was hearing him right.

"I don't think I got that?"

"You heard what I said."

He took another sip of the bottle. Offering me some and I told him yes. He grabbed a glass and poured me some.

"So why I never saw you before?" I asked.

"I used to live out here but now I'm living in Cali. I just came for the grand opening of our new club."

"Oh okay, so you guys are business partners. That's dope."

He randomly started to run his fingers through my hair.

"What it's something in my hair?" I asked.

"Nah, you saw what my hair felt like, so I wanted to see what yours felt like." he replied.

"Huh? For what?"

"For our babies."

The drink must have gone down the wrong pipe because I started coughing like a maniac. He just caught me completely off guard.

"Smooth *cough* talker *cough*." I tried to get out while still coughing. Vito just was patting my back laughing. Yes, laughing at me when I was practically dying. I was so embarrassed. First, the moan? Then, the coughing? Seriously Emerald? Get it together.

Drinking some more of my drink to soothe my throat he came closer to my face and asked me was I okay. Real close if you ask me.

"Yes, I'm okay."

"Oh, okay good, I thought I would've had to kiss my sleeping beauty back alive," he said to me while looking me straight in my eyes. Fuck it why not? If you want to kiss me alive then kiss me alive.

"Who said I'm alive yet?"

On that note he came closer to me. So close I smelt his breathe and even though he was drinking it still was a turn on. Just when we were about to kiss Yasmine and Yasir started arguing and yelling at each other. Saved by the fucking bell because I didn't know what I was just thinking.

"Why are you so worried about my pussy for?!" Yasmine yelled.

Here we go, I thought.

"Nobody worried about that shit you can keep it to yourself!" he yelled right back.

"SO, THE FUCK WHAT I'M A DANCER! I'm not your woman," Yasmine said while getting in his face.

"You damn right you not my woman because my woman wouldn't be a fucking dancer," Yasir said.

Nas got up with Candy's lipstick all over his neck with his hands in the air, "Ladiesssss, Fellassss why can't we just get along?"

I couldn't help but to start laughing. *They're so crazy.*

Yasmine looked upset and was getting her things to leave and since Trey left me, I needed a ride. I guess Vito saw I was getting ready to go.

"You're leaving?" He asked me.

"Yeah. I sort of need a ride".

"I can give you a ride," he said smiling.

With only one type of riding playing in my mind I wouldn't trust myself around him.

"Sorry I think Yasmine need someone to talk to. She seems upset," I knew Yasmine wouldn't dwell on this for long, but he didn't.

"Yeah, I understand go see about your home girl," he said.

I couldn't find my phone and I saw Yasmine getting further away.

"Shit! Where is my phone?"

Vito started to help me and finally he found it and passed it to me. I told him to tell Candy I left with Yasmine and said goodbye. Walking away he mouthed to me *"check your phone".* I didn't understand why but when I did, I saw a text message.

VITO: *Let me know when you get home.*

His slick ass had my phone the whole time. I told him okay and went to go find Yasmine.

Mia

There was a knock at my door, and I knew exactly who it was.

"Look what the wind done blew in," I said and rolled and eyes.

I was acting like I was upset but deep down I was jumping up and down with joy.

"Stop acting like you not excited to see me."

He was looking so good at the party tonight that's why I really went because deep down I knew I was going to be able to see him. He had a Gucci denim jacket with the matching jeans, a white Gucci polo shirt and some high-top construction boots looking thuggish and sexy ass ever.

"Shut up Trey with your rude ass!"

I knew he was going to come see me after that stunt Sasha pulled at the club. She was my best friend, but she was just so dumb at times. Every time she does something stupid, Trey comes knocking at my door. It wasn't supposed to happen like this but hey shit happens. Ever since she bragged to me how good his dick looked and felt I always questioned it in the back of mind. Which was really no harm doing but one day he came to my house looking for her and one thing lead to another. He was threatening me telling me that I knew where the fuck she was at and the whole nine yards. He made me call her, but she wasn't answering my phone calls. I had on a towel because I had just got out the shower and then the next thing I knew I was getting fucked from the back over my kitchen counter. Trey had the best dick I ever fucking had. Or maybe it was because it was dick that I wasn't supposed to be fucking. In the beginning I was feeling guilty but hey, can't go wrong with some good dick and money here and there. Sasha wasn't even just fucking with Trey the whole time so who knows if the baby is really his. That's why I never cared to bring it up to him.

"You were in on that shit tonight to huh?" He asked me.

"Maybe," I replied.

"Anything for some dick, right?" he laughed.

"Boy please you are not innocent your damn self."

"Y'all know what kind of nigga I am so I don't give a fuck,"

His cocky ass had the nerve to say.

"I forgot refresh my memory," I flirted.

I walked to my bedroom and Trey followed. My phone started to ring, and I saw it was Sasha calling. I wasn't going to answer but Trey insisted that I did.

"Girl, I think I fucked up," she said into the phone.

"What you mean?" I asked.

"Trey, he won't answer any of my phone calls," she said.

"Damn maybe he's busy."

"He's not busy! He's with that bitch!"

Little did she know I was the bitch he was with. Trey pulled down my panties and bent me over. He put on a condom and started giving me that dope dick. His dick felt so good I couldn't help but to moan.

"EW bitch what are you doing?!" She yelled into the phone.

I couldn't even respond so I hung up the phone.

"This dick must really be worth it huh?" He asked while pounding the shit out of my pussy. Hell, yeah it was. He knew my pussy was good too because he kept on coming back.

Yasmine

My arms were killing me from all these bags I was carrying. I made a lot of money last night so what better way to use it other than shopping? So here I was in Westfield Mall in Jersey having some retail therapy. Walking towards the parking lot of the mall I passed a jewelry store that caught my attention. The pieces looked so beautiful on the display, I just had to go and get a close for myself.

"Hello, how may I assist you today?" A worker asked me.

"Oh no I'm okay, just browsing," I chuckled.

This beautiful diamond choker caught my attention.

I would look so sexy on stage with that on, I thought.

I looked for the price tag and couldn't find one on it.

"Excuse me how much is this?" I asked the worker.

She came over and took it out the glass.

"Hmmm I don't see a price tag, the boss just stepped in so I will have him come and assist you," she told me as she went to the back to go and get him. I was sitting down for about three minutes when she informed me he was coming out.

Turning around I immediately started to laugh thinking it was a joke. He's the boss? Him out of all people?

"Sorry, I'm not interested anymore," I said getting up grabbing my bags.

"Yasmine," he called out.

I turned around to faced him.

"Can you come into my office please?" He asked me. I really didn't want to but whatever. I walked into his office and watched him close the door.

"I'm sorry about the other night," Yasir told me.

I knew he owned a jewelry store but why did it have to be this one?

"Sorry? It's nothing to be sorry about," I responded.

"Yes, what you do with your life is none of my concern," he said.

"Why do you even care anyway?" I asked him.

Changing the subject, he told me the price of the choker and asked me did I want to buy it.

"No, I was just window shopping," I told him.

"Would you like to see how it looks on you?" He asked.

Hey why not?

Walking towards me he moved my hair to the side and attached the choker around my neck. For some reason his touch felt different. It felt as if he was being very gentle with me. Walking towards the mirror in his office it was as if this piece was made just for me. Yasir and Nasir were twins but wasn't identical. With Nas being more brown skin or as Candy calls him, her *milk chocolate.* Yasir was more like dark chocolate. He also was tall, and you can tell he spends some of his time in the gym. He had a goatee that fully connected that was thick and dark. He was a good-looking man, but I felt because we never clicked, I never really noticed. I guess dark piercings eyes ran in the family because he had them also.

"Wow it's so beautiful," I told him.

"Yes, it looks very nice on you," He responded. This moment was awkward. He never really said anything kind to me. I told him to unhook the necklace so I can go. After he unhooked it, he placed it on his brown oak desk and walked closer to me. I felt like the room was closing in on us. Grabbing my hand, he apologized to me again. It was no room for me to move anywhere with the desk behind me with him in the front of me. I started to feel a little lightheaded. His phone started to ring thankfully. I was saved by the bell. I grabbed my bags and ran out of his office.

What was that all about?

Sasha

One Month Later

I didn't hear from Trey since the party. Maybe he was not dealing with me anymore. Well little does he know he can't be all the way done with me but, I'm going to let him think that for now. Out of the blue I grew overnight. My belly is now round and sticking out. I drove by places he'll be and asked around but it's like he vanished. Every number I would call him from would get blocked. Seems to me like he's jealous, but why would he be if he got a girlfriend, right? The only reason why I did that at the club was to get his attention and a whole month later he just disappeared. I felt my baby kick and it made me sadder because now I have no baby father at all. Fuck I should've thought this shit through! If he's not messing with me anymore, I needed to find a way to get money now. I have something saved up for a while but once that run out, I'll be assed out. I got tired of over thinking myself. I rubber my belly until I fell asleep.

1:30AM

Waking up out of my sleep, I thought I heard a noise but maybe I was bugging. *This baby be having me tripping at times*, I thought. I never knew pregnancy would ever be like this. Closing my eyes, I suddenly felt my feet getting dragged off the bed and I fell on to the floor. I started screaming but then the person covered my mouth with their hand.

SLAP!

"You thought that shit you did was cute right bitch?"

SLAP!

"DIDN'T I TELL YOU TO STOP PLAYING WITH ME?!"

The slaps were blinding my vision. I just started to feel hopeless.

"Please, stop I'm pregnant," I cried.

"Pregnant? No the fuck you not. I strap up every time and your ass better not be fucking anybody else," he said.

What? I know this is not Trey crazy fucking ass in my house fighting me over something that happened a month ago.

"Yes, the fuck I AM! And get your ass off me Trey. Why the fuck you came here trying to fight me? Go home to your woman!" I yelled. Suddenly the light came on and Trey looked at me confused.

"Sasha, what the fuck? When the hell did you get pregnant? Is this my baby?" He had the audacity to ask.

"I don't know when I got pregnant" I lied. I fucking knew but that's none of his business. "It must have happened a drunk night. I went a few months without my period but that always happens with my birth control, so I didn't think anything of it."

"Fuck! Fuck! Fuckkkk!" I heard him scream as he went towards the living room while I followed him. Most likely going to my bar to pour him some liquor.

"You knew I didn't want any fucking kids!" He yelled while taking a shot and then pouring another one.

"You act like it doesn't take two to make a baby as if I did it on my own!" I yelled and got into his face.

"Yeah I know. Shit! I just need to think!"

He took another shot. This fool was going to be drunk as hell. I went to the bathroom to look at my face because it was hurting badly. The right side of my face was swollen.

"Trey! Look what the fuck you did to my face!" I yelled at him as I walked up towards him.

"I told you to stop fucking playing with me."

"Playing with you? You have a woman and I didn't speak to you in a whole month!"

"Yeah, I had to teach your ass a lesson."

"No! I taught your ass a lesson!" Before I can even walk away, I felt his hands around my neck.

"Repeat yourself?" I felt like I couldn't breathe and was clawing at his hands so he can loosen up and then he tossed me on the couch.

"Keep playing with me Sasha. You are going to see."

What the fuck did I get myself into? Having no more energy left, I just cried my ass to sleep.

Opening my eyes, I felt Trey pulling down my satin shorts that I slept in. I wasn't even in the mood for sex right now.

"No Trey," I said as I tried to push him away.

"What you mean no? I thought this was my pussy," he said as he started to rub on my clit. I was so mad at my body because it was going against my mind. Trey was turning me on no matter what I was thinking.

"Hmmmm. No, I'm done with you," I moaned.

"You never could be done with me," he said and was fucking right. I don't know what he did to me but lord this man had a spell on me. He now had two fingers in my pussy and was sucking on my chest. He started slowly and then started to speed up. I started to grind on his fingers as I felt myself about to cum. I grabbed his head and kissed him as I came on his fingers. He got up and took his clothes off as I got up and took my top off.

"Where you going? Get on top of this dick."

"To go get a condom Trey."

"For fucking what? You already pregnant."

We never had raw sex before no matter how much I tried to. I knew it was going to feel so fucking good. Walking back over to him he sat on the couch and I got on top of him. Slowly putting his dick inside of me to adjust to the size.

"Damn Sasha," he moaned. I knew it felt as good as it did to me, to him. I started to go a little faster up and down on his dick.

"Trey you feel so good baby. I love you."

"I know you do. Now cum on this dick baby. Yeah ride that shit and you better not stop." I rode his dick until he came inside of my pussy. If I wasn't pregnant already, I was going to be.

Trey was out cold snoring right after he came. His phone kept ringing. I grabbed it to turn it off saw that it was Emerald calling. *Bitch*. Then a thought came to mind. She didn't know about me before. Well she was going to know about me now. I took her number down and turned his phone off. Getting in bed I kissed him and closed my eyes. I was a fool in love.

Emerald

I smiled as I read the text Vito sent me "*when you going to stop playing and let me see you?*" Even though Trey and I are going through things now it doesn't mean I should stray. Yes, I know at the club we were about to kiss and that's another reason why I'm not going to be alone with him. It almost happened once, and I feel like it can happen again.

ME: *Soon. Before you leave, I promise.*

I was lying. It did feel good to have somebody to talk to though. Trey has been getting better for a whole month now, surprisingly. We were going on dates more often and the insecurities and accusing me of things stopped. He was being nicer to Candy too. She didn't care because she still didn't like him. I was on my way to the shop to get my nails done. I was dodging Vito fine ass and made sure Nas wasn't coming to the shop today with him.

Pulling up to Candy's I got out the car and walked into the shop. Candy was doing a weave on a client of hers.

"Hey girl," I said as I walked up to her and gave her a kiss on her cheek.

"Hey Em, you look cute today!" she complimented me.

I had on a cute green sleeveless dress and some black sandals that tie all the way up to my knees.

"Really? I thought I looked fat," I said looking in one of the mirrors.

"Girl you look perfectly fine shut the hell up," Candy said.

I went to Simone station and sat down. Simone was one of the nail technicians and my favorite. I never had any complaints when she did my nail that's why I was a certified customer of hers.

"So how do you want them today?" She asked.

"Hmm I don't really know surprise me," I replied.

"Are you sure?"

"Yes, girl I have faith in you," I laughed.

An hour later she was finally done with my nails and Candy didn't have any more clients. She was waiting for Nas to come and get her, and she didn't want me to leave her alone, so I waited with her. Nas called her and told her he was on his way.

"Ask him if he's with Vito?" I whispered.

"Babe are you with your cousin? Scary Mary over here would like to know," Candy said.

She shook her head no. Feeling relieved I got up to go and use the bathroom. After using the bathroom, I applied some of my lip gloss on.

Knock! Knock!

"Somebody's in here!" I yelled.

Knock! Knock! Knock! Knock!

"I said somebody is in here!" I yelled as I swung the door open.

"Uh oh hi Vito," I said surprised to see him obviously.

I'm going to kill Candy and Nas. Vito walked into the bathroom and locked the door. He had on a grey suit that fitted him to a T. I never saw him dressed like this before, so it caught me off guard, but he did inform me that was a businessman. His dreads were still neat from when I did them and it also looked like he just gotten a shape up. Looking at his cufflinks, they were shining so bright. I felt like Alicia Keys in her video to the song "You Don't Know My Name". He had me willing to risk my job and use some milk and cream for him, just like Alicia felt.

"So, this is what I have to do to see you?" he pressed.

"Oh, ummm no I was just about to text you," I lied.

"Why are lying? What, you scared of me?" he asked.

Hell yeah! I thought.

"Scared of you? Why would I fear you?"

"Because you act like you scared to see a nigga. Dinner, movies, something," He said.

"You know I have a man."

"Okay and who said anything about that? So, hanging out is a problem?" he asked.

I knew he thought he was slick. The shit that he be texting to me, yeah okay I knew he wanted to do more than just *hang out* and I felt guilty as hell because I did too.

"No, it's not Vito," I replied.

"Okay well now when I tell you next time, I don't want to hear no excuses okay. We don't have to be in a private setting, I just want to spend some time with you before I go," he said.

"Okay, I promise friend," I laughed. Reaching towards to the bathroom door I tried to open it, but he grabbed my hand.

"You can't give your *friend* a hug before you dip?"

Oh boy. Turning around I gave him a hug and tried to move but he was still grabbing on to me.

"You know this is our first hug?" he asked smiling.

"Yes. I know it is," I smiled back.

This was not a normal hug. Hugs aren't supposed to feel this good. Looking at me he let me go and stared into my eyes. It felt like my feet were glued to the floor because no matter how much I wanted to, I couldn't move. Coming closer and closer, our heads were now actually touching one another. Butterflies fluttered through my body being so close to him. This is what I didn't want because something was bound to happen being alone with him. The way his words flowed out of his perfect shaped lips; his dark skin tone can easily make a woman fall in love. No marks, no scars, just the perfect sculpture you can easily start to crave.

"And you know this is our first kiss," he said kissing my lips catching me off guard. He kissed me!

"Umm Vito wait," I told him trying to stop him.

"And you know this is our second kiss," He said and kissed me again. I felt my knees getting weak. This was so bad. I shouldn't be doing this or even in the bathroom with him. What the hell is going on? Turning me around to face the mirror he got behind me.

"You look so beautiful. I love how green looks on you, my Emerald." I was blushing so hard my cheeks were hurting.

"And this is the first time I kissed on your neck," he said and then proceed to plant soft, soothing kisses on my neck. As a natural reaction I arched my back enjoying the feeling, soon after I felt his dick expanding on my ass. "You see what you doing to me?" he asked.

What the heck? I wasn't doing shit. I just wanted to use the bathroom in peace. Grabbing my hands and spreading them on the sink he put his hands-on top of mines and kissed my neck again. His dreads smelled so good.

"And this is the first time you felt my dick on your ass. You like that?"

No, No, No, No, I thought.

"Yes," instead came out of my mouth.

Shit!

"We are hanging out next week and I don't want to hear anything," He said opening the bathroom door and walking away. Lord this man was trouble! Giving myself time to try and look normal. I counted to twenty before I opened the bathroom door. Walking towards the front of the shop I saw Vito sitting down on the phone staring at me with nothing but lust in his eyes. I stuck my middle finger up at Nas and Candy as I walked towards the door.

"Vito, what you did to my friend?" I heard Candy asked.

"Nothing yet," I heard Vito say before the door closed.

For about two days now a private number kept calling me and every time I would answer the caller would just hang up. Finally, I guess they decided to just text me.

1456-678-9909: *Leave my man alone bitch!*

ME: *Who is this?*

1456-678-9909: *Ask Trey he knows exactly who this is.*

I called the number, but it was from a text free app. I didn't even feel like responding. I went to my contacts and called Trey.
"Yo?" He answered.
"What bitch you got playing on my phone?" I asked him.
"What that fuck you talking about?" he asked.
"A girl is texting me saying to leave you alone and how you her man," I said.
"And you believe that? Don't call my phone on any stupid shit like that," he said and hung up.
I kept calling him and he wouldn't even answer. This nigga made me want to pull my fucking hair out. My phone started to ring, and I ran to my phone thinking it was Trey, but it was Candy.
"Yeah?" I answered.

"Why you sound like that? What that bum ass nigga did now?" she asked.

"I think he is cheating on me Candyyyyy," I cried.

"What? What happened?" she asked me.

I gave her the rundown of everything that happened.

"And he hung up on you? As if it was a problem with you asking him? How dare he? Bum ass nigga! Fuck him Emerald! Seriously!" She yelled as I cried even more.

VITO: *You ready?*

Shit I forgot all about Vito. I wasn't even in the mood anymore. I just cried myself to sleep. I really hope Trey wasn't cheating on me.

I finally got myself together. I wasn't going to spend my day in bed crying over a man who brought me so much grief. I told Vito I was ready, but Candy was going to come get me instead because I didn't want to cause any problems with Vito and Trey. Candy told me she was downstairs, so I locked up and went to her car.

"Well hello sexy," Candy jokes.

I decided to wear a red leather skirt, a blue denim jean jacket with my shoulders free with some cute white sandals.

"You don't even know where we are going," she said.

"Yeah, but I do look sexy right?"

"Remember the barbecue we went to when you first met Trey? Well that's where we are going. I hope your feet feel fine," she laughed

"Ha-ha! Real funny. I always got a pair of flip flops with me," I said. "But seriously, what if Trey be there?"

"I doubt it. Him and Nas barely speak anymore," she responded.

"True."

We arrived at the barbecue and I was feeling a mixture of so many different emotions. So many things changed over time. When I first came here to meet up with Trey, we were so irresistible in that little time. Then, things just suddenly started to change. He went from my knight and shining armor to someone I barely recognized. Well I guess it's the way of life. All relationships aren't meant to last, they're just meant to get you prepared for your next one.

"Baby, come outside to come get us," Candy said when Nas answered the phone.

"Why don't we just walk in?" I asked her.

"Because I want all these hoes to see the trophy my man is going to be stunting on his arm," Candy flipping her hair.

A few minutes later we saw Nas in front of the house, so we got out the car and starting walking towards him. I saw him laughing with someone but couldn't see who it was. Suddenly, Vito came from behind him. Vito was so damn fine. Even when I didn't try to be mesmerized by his looks, I just couldn't help it. His dreads were hanging freely, wavy from the braids they were in with a little messy look. He made that look so good. *Maybe he should wear his hair like that more often. Wait why am I even thinking about this?*

Being so into one another like usually, Candy and Nas was in their own world.

I saw Vito walking closer to me.

"Hi Vi-" before I can even finish his name I tripped on apparently thin air and fell right into his arms, his strong big brown sexy arms. Candy was just looking at me smirking away.

"Sorry I must have tripped on something," I laughed wiping away at the imaginary wrinkles on my skirt.

"Right into my arms? That must be a sign baby."

"Quit it Vito," I said hitting him on the shoulder.

"I'm all for the game baby I don't want to quit," he said.

"I already told you my situation."

"So, you don't want to be situated?" He asked.

"Vito…"

"Okay, okay fine," he said putting his hands up defeated.

I didn't know where me and Trey stood so I didn't even want to make a promise to anyone when I didn't even know what is was that I wanted to do. Ms. Yvonne cooked the food here so first thing first I was going to get me a plate or two before I started to party! She should really open her own restaurant. Her food was the best I've tasted yet.

Two hours later, and the party was still going on. People I saw from around the way was here and people I've never even seen a day in my life, too many people might I add. Candy and I were dancing with one another while the DJ was playing old school reggae. I didn't really know how to dance but with a few drinks in me, I thought I was the whining queen.

"Girl, Vito is coming this way right now! Don't turn around…" Candy said.

Before she can even finish her sentence, I felt arms wrap around my waist. She must have told me too late because he appeared rather quickly. I didn't even have to turn around because I knew it was him from his hypnotizing cologne he wore. It's like whenever he would leave my presence, I would still smell it days later. I smelled liquor on his breathe so I knew he was drinking. Vito and I drinking together was not a good thing at all.

"So, are you going to dance on me like I just saw you dancing when I was standing over there," he asked kissing my neck. One of the feelings I wished I felt again since the bathroom.

"I don't dance," I replied trying to turn around but, he wouldn't let me. All I kept thinking about was if somebody Trey knew saw us.

"Well, let me teach you."

We were far off in the corner because I didn't want to be out in the open when we first arrived, so I told Candy let's chill over here. I honestly was trying to hide from Vito but low and behold he found me. "I'm Still in Love with You Boy" by Sean Paul started to play. His hands went from my waist to the inside of my thighs.

"Put your hands on the gate," he whispered in my ear.

You know you make me holla boy you make me shout
But I can't get your tenderness

Still I can't get you off my mind

"What is it about you baby?" Vito whispered in my ear finishing off the verse. He started to move and wine his waist behind me and lord forgive me, but all I could think about at this moment was if he can move like this in the bedroom. I didn't even know he could dance.

"Move with me," he told me.

I'm still in love with you boy?
Well I'm a hustler and a player
And you know I'm not a stayer
I'm still in love with you boy?

I don't know if it was the drinks but all that shyness I had went right through the window. You would've thought it was Vito and I in the dance video. He started to kiss on my neck again and I felt what he had tucked away inside of his pants poking at my backside.

"This is the second time I felt your dick on my ass," I told him.

I didn't know where that boldness came from and Vito looked like he didn't either because he seemed shocked, I said that out of my mouth.

"I have to go to the bathroom," I snapped out of it quick and nearly busted my ass trying to get away from Vito.

Walking to the bathroom, wherever it was I bumped right into Maine. If Maine was here that only meant one thing, Trey was here. I didn't have to wonder to long because I saw Trey coming right towards me. He yanked my arm pulling me towards him.

"So first you accuse me of some shit and now you out here being a hoe. I should slap the shit out of you!" He yelled. Making a scene like he always does.

"Trey, get off of me!" I pulled my arm away from him.

"You want to test me?" He asked with fire in his eyes.

"Trey, get off of her," Nas told him.

"Or else what?" Trey questioned.

"Who the fuck you talking to?" Candy asked Trey.

All of this was going bad. Soon become worst because I saw Vito walking this way with an angry look on his face.

"Candy, mind your business baby," Nas told her calmly.

"Nas, you a funny nigga. You got my girl out here with your cousin. What you trying to be matchmaker of the year? Clown ass nigga!" Trey yelled.

"Definitely a clown move," Rah had the nerve to say.

"Didn't anybody hook me up with nobody, If you were doing your job right—" Vito started to say.

"Vito!" I yelled cutting him off.

"Oh, so you pillow talking with niggas?" Trey asked looking at me with pure disgust, the nerve of this nigga. I can't believe him. I didn't have time for all this commotion anymore, so I just told Candy I was leaving, and Trey followed behind me with Maine and Rah. The whole way home he wouldn't shut up, but it all went in one ear and out the other.

Yasmine

It was Friday night and Passion was jumping. I knew I was going to get paid tonight. Jay has been MIA recently which is always a good thing. I loved the money and the thrill just being here. Taking a double shot of Henny to get into the mood because it was about to be my time to get on stage. Everybody loved me and all the females hated that. Instead of going against me, they should jump on my bandwagon so I can show them a few moves. They rather envy me, more money for me.

"I know you're going to kill it tonight Bambi," A random guy came up to me and whispered. Wasn't no way in hell I was going to use my real name with these creeps.

"Let me get a Henny and pineapple," I heard someone next to me request from the bartender. Turning around I saw it was Yasir. I rolled my eyes and walked away. If he had a problem with strippers so much, why was he here?

"I know this is who you all been waiting for. Don't act the fuck up when she get on stage because you will get kicked out! Its Bambi babyyyyyy!"

I heard the DJ start to play "Ssh" by Tevin Campbell. The people loved when I danced to that song. I walked on to the stage and saw so many faces. Only one face stood out to me, Yasir. He always had so much shit to say but let's see what he going to say after tonight.

Shhh, break it down
I don't want nobody else to hear the sounds
This love is a private affair
Interrupt the flow, no they better not dare
Shhh, we got to break it on down

˜ I walked to the pole to swing around it. Climbing up the pole I did a few tricks and came down into a split. The crowd went crazy and money started flying everywhere. I starred Yasir right in his eyes and took off my blue shiny top.

Massaging my breast, I started to play with my nipples. I got on my knees and crawled to the end of the stage. Getting on my back his eyes were still on me. If you ask me, it looked like he was staring at me with lust. Taking off my blue thong I opened my legs and start to rub on my pussy. I faked moaned and closed my eyes.

> *In the daytime, uh, uh, I think not*
> *I'd rather do you after school*
> *Like some homework, am I getting' you hot?*
> *In my bedroom? No, 'cause then we have to stop*
> *Please don't stop*

Opening my eyes, I saw Yasir was gone. *Hump! Too much for him to handle I see,* I thought. Closing my eyes again getting back into the groove I felt myself getting yanked up. *What the fuck?* I opened my eyes and saw Yasir with an angry face.

"Come the fuck on! Get your ass up," he said.

"Excuse me? Get the fuck off me!" I yelled.

"You heard what the fuck I said now let's go!"

I was so fucking confused. What the hell was going on? Was it Candy? Was she hurt?

"I'm going to be waiting by your car and don't take long," he said and went towards the front of the club.

"Girl, was his fine ass your man?" One of the nosey strippers asked me.

"Mind your business!" I yelled and went towards the back to get my shit. Not only did he embarrass me, but he made me miss out on a lot of fucking money today. I couldn't believe this. Grabbing my things, I walked out the club to see Yasir and I guess one of his friends by my car.

"What the fuck was that all about?" I yelled walking towards him.

"Give me your car keys," he demanded.

"What? Did you not hear what the fuck I just said?"

"Did you not hear what the fuck I JUST SAID? Now give me the keys," he said. I gave them to him, and he gave it to his friend.

"He's going to follow behind us in your car get in," he said

And with that he went to the driver seat of his car and I got in the passenger seat. It was quiet for the rest of the ride besides me questioning him over and over about what was going on. Fed up, I just stopped questioning him. He ruined the fuck out of my night. He pulled up to my apartment and I tried to open the car door, but it was locked.

"You need to find a new job," he said.

"Excuse me?"

"You heard me. You can't strip anymore. Find something else to do."

"Who are you to be telling me what the fuck I can't do?"

"Your man and as my woman I don't want YOU to be stripping anymore".

"*My man?* What? Is this a joke?" I started laughing.

"Yeah your man and if I hear about you stripping again It's going to be a problem Yasmine. I'm going out of town for a few days and I don't want any problems when I get back," he said. I was so confused, and he was giving me a headache.

He went in his pockets and gave me two stacks out of it.

"Here this should make up for tonight." He grabbed the back of my head and tongued me down.

"Don't be hardheaded and get fucked up. I'm going to call you in a little."

I got out the car and he smacked me on my ass. He waited until I got in my building and sped off.

What the fuckkkk? Oh hell no! One of those bitches spiked my drink tonight and when I find out who it was, I was going to fuck them up! Because there's no way this just happened.

"He did what?!" Candy yelled.

Yes of course I'm going to tell my girls about this. They were shocked as hell just like I was! It's been a few days and I still can't believe it! Candy knew firsthand how me and Yasir relationship was so she couldn't believe it also.

"Wow so maybe he was mad because this whole time he liked you…." Emerald said stating the obvious.

"If he liked me this whole time why didn't his big-headed ass just say something instead of arguing with me all the time," I said.

"Well you use to start with him most of time," Emerald projected.

"Well I didn't like him!"

"Didn't? So, you like him now?" Candy asked.

"I don't know!"

I really didn't know. Everything happened so fast. I used to hate him last week but now it's a different ball game. He was still out of town but some way he found my number and we started texting and talking faithfully. He was really a cool dude too, which surprised the hell out of me. We always had something to talk about and he was so sweet. I would get good morning texts every morning and I never had that before. We were taking it slow and I was enjoying whatever it is that we had going on.

"So, you're not going to strip anymore?" Candy asked.

"Well I don't know about that. I need money for my bills and I just can't stop like that" I said.

"I thought you said Yasir said -" Emerald begins to ask.

"Yeah I know what he said but he doesn't have to know!" I said cutting her off.

Candy started to shake her head.

"What?!" I asked rolling my eyes.

"I don't think you should go against him. If he's anything like his brother it's not going to be a pretty site," She said.

"Well are you going to pay my bills? No? Exactly!" I yelled answering my own question.

Trying to change the tone of where this conversation was going Emerald got up and walked next to me and said, "Well Yasmine and Yasir does sound cute together." We all started laughing.

"Yeah Ms. Vito," I said, and she immediately started to frown.

"What happened?" I asked.

"He doesn't talk to me anymore I guess," she shrugged.

"Why not, still from the barbecue?" Candy asked.

"Well, I guess he got tired of playing games with me and cut me off for good. I told him I'm with someone and he just must respect that. That don't mean we can't be friends though. He didn't even give me enough time," she said.

"Why are you still even holding on to him?" Candy asked rolling her eyes referring to Trey.

"It's better easier said than done," Emerald replied.

I honestly thought she can do so much better than Trey also. He put her through so much. That's one of my biggest fears is to be with a man and he have me looking so dumb. I hated that about Emerald. She was beautiful and successful but wasted time with him.

"UGHHHHH! I think I need to change my number," Emerald said.

"That number keeps texting you?" I asked.

"Yes, she even said her name is Sasha. I stopped bringing it up to Trey because that just starts an argument between us," she said.

"Sasha? What if this is real Emerald what are you going to do?" Candy asked.

"I don't know at all. I just pray all the time it's not," she said.

Poor Emerald. Maybe this was a sign she needed to let Trey dog ass roam.

"Well with all this playing around "Sasha" is doing. If she is real and knew about you when I find her, I'm going to whip her fucking ass!" I yelled. Everybody knew I didn't play when it came to somebody that I love.

Okay, so this trying to find a job thing wasn't working. It been almost two months and I'm running out of patience. Stripping is all I know and I'm damn sure good at it so what's the problem? Yasir basically was giving me a job at the shop but I didn't accept it. I told Yasir I was going out tonight, so he doesn't think nothing of it. He went out of town again and he's not coming back until tomorrow anyway so he wouldn't have a clue. I was getting mad love, and everybody missed me even though it was just two months. See stripping is me! I wish everybody would understand that.

"Yeah, I saw her the other day she done went and got knocked up, "Cinnamon said. All these bitches do is gossip in the locker room all damn day.

"Yup that's why that hoe haven't been here. Starting a family and shit," Bubbles replied.

"Who y'all talking about?" Diamond asked.

"Sasha," Cinnamon said.

Sasha? I thought. The conversation me and the girls had a while back suddenly came to mind.

"Sasha from where?" I asked.

"You don't know her," Cinnamon said waving me off. Remember one of the bitches that I said that envy me? Yup she was the head runner up.

"The one that use to work here with us. I think her stripper name was Hypnotic," My girl Bubbles said. Bubbles was cool that's why I fucked with her.

"Ohhh I know who you are talking about," I said to her and rolled my eyes at Cinnamon.

"Anyway, I heard her dude is paid too! But supposedly Sasha is his side piece because he got a girl at home," I heard Cinnamon say while walking out of the room.

Bitches run they mouth too much.

After doing my set I sat at the bar and chilled with Bubbles. We was just catching up and she is letting me know what's been going on here since I wasn't here for a while.

"Would you happen to have a picture of Sasha?" I asked her.

"Yeah I have her Instagram. Why was sup?" She asked.

"I just wanted to make sure I knew exactly who you guys were talking about."

Bitch don't worry about why!

She showed me Sasha and I remember her ass. I didn't see her in a long time here. When Bubbles wasn't looking, I took down her Instagram so it can be in my recent searches.

"Bambi room three private dancing," Rick the owner came and told me.

"How much?" I asked.

"Eight thousand so hurry your ass up!" He said.

I went to go freshen up and walked into the room. It was very dark so I couldn't see who the person was.

"Any song of choice?" I asked.

"Yeah," that voice sounded familiar, but I didn't pay it any mind.

"Which is?" I asked.

I got close and when he turned around, I felt my stomach in my ass. He said he wouldn't be back until tomorrow.

"What did I tell you?" He asked me as he got closer and closer. I backed up until my back was against the wall.

"It's not what you think," I said.

"It's not what I think? So, what the fuck is it then? I told you ass I didn't want you stripping anymore!" He yelled.

"You didn't even give me time to save up some more money or anything! That's not fair!" I yelled right back.

"Why the fuck you showing people what belong to me now? You hard of listening?" He asked.

"No," I mumbled.

"Huh? I didn't hear you. You always got so much to say. Speak the fuck up now!"

"I said no!"

"Oh okay. I was hoping you was. Now I know you basically just don't give a fuck," he said and walked towards the door.

"Yasir wait! Let me explain," I said and grabbed him.

"Isn't shit to explain. I'm, not trying to knocking your hustle do you."

And with that he walked out the door and left me stuck looking stupid.

Shit!

Nas

    I was waiting for my cousin Vito to come meet me at the club so we can have a meeting. I'm so glad I turned my life around and went legit with this club business. It wasn't nothing like getting money living the fast life like I'm used to, but it wasn't bad at all. Me and Trey use to be in the streets heavy. Well Trey is still doing his thing and big ups to that man. Ever since I started dealing with the clubs me and his relationship wasn't the same. I get it when we got money together, we got *moneyyy* together, but I didn't want to live like that anymore. Always looking over my shoulder and having to show examples to people so they knew better to fuck with me. Don't get it twisted though, they still know better, but I can rest peacefully at night and don't have to worry about cops kicking down my door.

"Baby why you left and didn't say bye to me?" My baby Candy asked me.

She face timed me when she woke up and noticed that I was gone. I had her ass spoiled rotten. I wasn't even the type to be settling down but her sexy ass did something to me. From the first night I met her I wanted her, but she was drunk and seemed to not be in the right state of mind, so I let her get away. But when I saw her again? I had to stake my claim.

"I didn't want to wake you baby I kissed you before I left though."

"That doesn't count because I don't remember," she pouted.

"Okay so when I see you the first thing, I'm going to do is kiss your lips," I told her, and she started smiling.

"What lips you talking about?" she asked.

Her nasty ass.

"Whichever lips it is that you want me to kiss," I told her as Vito walked through the door.

"Whoa whoa whoa! What did I walk into?" he asked and gave me a pound.

"Heyyyyy cousin," She said.

That's another thing I liked about Candy. She wasn't all stuck up like most females are. She was a real down to earth person.

"Was sup Can," he replied.

"Why you do my girl like that?" She asked.

"Because she play to many games. Either she on my team or not," He said and seemed a little aggravated about that.

"You know she stuck on that bum ass-" I cut Candy off because she was starting to talk her shit.

"Baby I'm going to chop it up with Vito and call you back," I told her.

"Okay babe love you," She said.

"Love you too," I told her and hung up.

Two hours later our meeting was finally over, and I was ready to relax. I called over one of the bottle girls Synthia over.

"Bring a bottle over of Henny and some Red Bull's over," I told her.

"Okay boss man whatever you want," she said while licking her lips and walked away.

"Seems like little Synthia got a thing for you," Vito said

"You think so?" I asked.

"Okay boss man," he mocked, and we started laughing.

Shit maybe she do. If she knew like I knew she would get rid of that crush real fast because Candy was a beast when it came to me and didn't have no problem putting any of these hoes in check.

Vito looked at his phone and shook his head.

"Emerald ass don't get it," He said.

"What happened?"

"She is texting me asking how I just up and disappear like that. I'm letting her have what she want. Either she was fucking with me or not. I gave her enough time but, it's always something about her Nigga that's obviously dogging her and she's so blind and can't see that shit. I'm not going to talk down on the next man to her though because that's not even my style," He said.

I felt what he was saying though. I always wondered why Trey was like that but did so much to get her. Maybe it was an ego thing, who knows. Synthia came back with the drinks and I thanked her.

"Anything for you, boss man," she said and walked away.

"Yeah that bitch want the dick," Vito laughed.

Well her ass wasn't getting it, so she better stay right in her fucking place.

"So, you going to do it when y'all come down to California?" Vito asked.

"Yup I think I'm ready," I told him.

I was going to finally propose to Candy. She thought we was going down there just to see Vito and about the other club and I was going to let her think that. My baby was going to be shock and I couldn't wait to see her reaction.

"That's dope bro I'm proud of you," he said as we poured our drinks.

Walking inside my housé I knew I was fucked up. Me and Vito finished that whole bottle.

"Vito why you let him get this drunk!" Candy yelled. Everybody knew I wasn't a drinker and couldn't hang.

"Don't blame me, blame the Henny," he said laughing feeling it too.

"Vito take your ass downstairs and get in the shower y'all stink!" She yelled as she grabbed me and took me upstairs. She undressed me and put me in the tub while washing me up. My baby was so sweet.

"Get in the tub with me," I told her.

"I took a shower already tonight baby," she said.

"I didn't ask all that I said get in with me," I told her, and she took off her night clothes. I loved seeing her chocolate ass naked still till this day.

"I missed you baby," I told her and kissed her.

"Eww baby I taste the Henny on your breathe," she said.

"So, what that mean? I can't get no kisses from my baby?" I asked her.

"Baby you can get all the kisses you want," she told me.

I grabbed her washcloth and started to clean her.

"Tell me about your day baby," I said to her and she started to tell me about the changes she wanted to make to the shop and all the shop gossip. I loved to see how she was so involved with everything in the shop. She was so thankful for having her shop.

"Did you ever find out earlier?" I asked her.

"Find out what?" She questioned.

"Which lips it was that you wanted me to kiss?"

"You drunk baby."

"What the fuck that mean? Now did you find out?" I asked her.

"I wanted a kiss on the lips that's on my face," she said.

"Oh, I was hoping the other lips," I replied and gave her a kiss.

"I didn't say that you couldn't kiss me there either," she said with lust in her eyes. I grabbed her and put her up on the edge of the tub.

"Baby let's get in the bed I'm going to fall," she said.

"No, you not I got you," I told her as I grabbed her and went headfirst. I started giving her clit pecks.

"That's how you want the kisses baby?" I asked her.

"No," she said and grabbed my head tighter.

"How you want them? You want some tongue too baby?"

"Yes daddy," she moaned. I started to add some tongue with the kisses. She started grinding on my face. I started to fuck her tight pussy with my tongue.

"Ohhh Nas eat this pussy baby," she moaned. That's exactly what I did too. I was eating the shit out of her pussy. I felt her wetness running down my chin.

"You going to make me cum baby," she moaned with her legs shaking.

"I didn't tell you, you could cum yet."

"Baby I don't think I can hold ittttt."

"Yes, the fuck you can. You only cum when I tell you too."

Her eyes was closed tightly. I knew she was trying to concentrate on not Cuming. When I felt like she had enough I told her she could cum and that's exactly what she did. All over my face, it felt like I was drowning. I liked when she waited because that's when that shit got super wet.

"Now come get on this drunk dick," I told her.

My shit was hard as a fucking brick. Candy got on top of me and started riding the shit out of my dick. I grabbed her right breast and sucked on it while she moaned in my ear telling me how much she love me.

"You going to give me my baby girl, right?" I asked her.

"Yes babyyy," she moaned.

"Damn Candy slow down baby," I moaned.

She always got excited when she was on top making me look like a one-minute man. I couldn't help it though, that shit felt too good.

"No baby take this pussy. Cum for me baby," she moaned and started sucking on my neck. She knew that was my spot.

"Fuck Candy damn baby I'm Cumming," I said as I released inside of her.

"Oh yes baby me too," she said as she started Cumming too.

"I love you Nas," she said to be out of breath.

"I love you too baby."

Yasir

YASMINE: *Can you come over please? I'm sorry.*

She been sending me messages like this for weeks now. She obviously needed to get taught a lesson because she didn't listen. I told her ass to stop fucking stripping and she went behind my back and did the shit anyway. I came a day earlier because I wanted to surprise her ass and she in the fucking club showing everybody MY pussy. I been feeling Yasmine for a while now. Everybody thought I didn't like her when I was just disappointed that's why. She was smart and it was so much more than she can be doing besides shaking her ass in the club. Talking about she needed money to save. I knew she had money saved up so her ass shouldn't even have waste her time lying to me.

I got to her crib and knocked on the door.

"I can't believe you finally came!" She said and hugged me.

"Yeah why you wanted me to come so bad. Was sup?" I asked her.

"Can you stop being mad at me? Baby I miss you."

"I can't fuck with liars," I told her.

"I know I'm sorry I won't do it again," she pleaded.

"How I know you telling the truth?"

"Because I am. I understand now," she said.

"Well that's all you wanted me to come over for. I'm about to leave," I told her and walking towards the door.

"Wait. Yasir!" She yelled following behind me.

"What happened? I know it's not the big bad wolf Yasmine begging."

She looked like she was about to cry. I never seen this side of her before.

"Can I get a kiss?" She asked me.

I wanted to kiss the hell out of her, but I was still mad at her. People might think I'm dragging it but I'm not. I'm not trying to control her or anything, I just see so much more in her.

"Nah I'm good luv," I told her.

She didn't listen anyway because she came up to me and started to kiss me. It's like my hands had a mind of its own because they automatically went to her ass. She had on a black silk robe with I think nothing underneath because I felt her bare ass. It felt so soft and round. She stopped kissing me and looked me in my eyes. Her round face was so beautiful. I loved the shit out of her full lips. Truth be told, when I saw her ass in the club and everybody drooling over her I couldn't take it anymore. She knew what she was doing when she was staring at me doing all that freak nasty shit. That's exactly why I dragged her ass off the stage. Out of all the strippers I saw in my life, they never made me feel like that, so I knew if I felt like that, imagine how everybody else felt seeing her. Well they wasn't going to see her ass anymore because I don't like to share.

"Yasir. Believe me. I promise," she said and kissed me again. This time my hands were still moving with a mind of its own, went to her pussy and just like I expected she didn't have any panties on.

"Why you walking around the crib with no panties on? Who you are expecting?" I asked her.

"I have on a robe silly. It's no sense of me having any panties on," she laughed.

I backed her up onto the wall and grabbed one of her legs and wrapped them around my waist. My left hand grabbed her butt while my right hand was massaging her pussy. She was getting wetter and wetter.

"You going to be a good girl and listen to what I say now?" I asked her.

"Yes, baby I swear," she moaned.

I put one of my fingers into her pussy. *Damn this shit is tight,* I thought. I put another one in while still massaging her clit. My fingers was drenched with her wetness. She started to moan in my ear while sucking on my earlobe. Shit, that was feeling good, but I wasn't going to let up that easy. She started grinding on my fingers I felt her pussy jumping so I knew she was about to climax.

Just like I thought she came on my fingers and I took them out of her pussy and sucked all her juices off.

"Well I don't believe you," I said and walked away leaving her stuck looking confused. She thought she had control of this situation but she damn sure didn't. She going to learn not to go against what the fuck I tell her ass.

Yasmine

"I told you," Candy said.

"Bitch I don't want to hear that right now!" I yelled.

"Well he still not answering your messages?" She asked.

The answer was no! It's been a week since her came to see me surprisingly, and I still didn't hear from him. I didn't think he would take it this far being that we haven't been dating for too long, but I got use to talking to him every day and I missed him so much. I apologized and wasn't in the club since. He didn't block me because all my messages said delivered but I guess he didn't care to respond.

Grabbing my phone, I saw that I had a notification and I hoped like hell it was Yasir. But as my luck have it, it was just Instagram. Going to the search bar on Instagram, I was about to put in Yasir Instagram to see what he been up to, but I stumbled across somebody else's. *Therealhypnotic.* I was so caught up with Yasir and his little attitude I totally forgot about this. I went to her Instagram zoning Emerald and Candy out. She was a pretty girl and maybe I was being dramatic but when I heard the name Sasha, I immediately thought of the Sasha that was texting Emerald phone. I didn't see nothing out of the ordinary. Going back up, one picture stood out. She had a picture in a Red Benz with beige leather seats. Now Trey was the only Nigga I knew that owned a car like that because he got it custom made like that. Okay maybe someone else can have a car like that but I highly doubt it.

"Emerald. Trey still have that Red Benz?" I questioned.

"Yeah he never letting that car go, that's his baby," she answered.

"Are the seats still beige?" I asked her.

"Yes Yasmine, why?" She asked.

I handed her my phone and she looked stuck like her mind was going crazy. Candy walked over to where Emerald was at and grabbed the phone.

"Oh no the fuck he didn't!" She yelled.

Emerald still looked like she was in the zone. Suddenly tears started falling from her eyes.

"He said he didn't know a Sashaaaa," she cried.

I felt so bad for her. I went into my room and threw on some leggings and my boots! I was going to whip a bitch ass! I knew they said she was pregnant, but I didn't see no pregnant shit on Instagram, so I kept that part to myself. I knew exactly where she lived because I knew exactly who she was. When I got back to the living room Emerald was crying like she lost her best friend and Candy was rubbing her back.

"Come on y'all," I said putting Vaseline on my face.

"Where you are going?" Candy asked.

"To go see if that is really her. She used to work in the club, so I know her," I said.

"No, I don't think we should do anything until I talk to Trey," Emerald dumb ass had the nerve to say.

"Let's go now!!!" I screamed.

Candy jumped up and grabbed her bag and Emerald got up looking like a sad puppy as we walked towards the door. I hoped and prayed the pregnancy rumor was a lie.

Emerald

I can't believe Trey would do this to me. Why me? Just why? He argued me down about accusing him of Sasha being real and all along she was. Was I that naive? I can't believe I let this slip right through my fingers.

"This is it," Yasmine said and got out the car with Candy.

"Come on Emerald," Candy said.

I never thought my life would come to this. I didn't even want to be here, but I knew they wouldn't take no for an answer.

"SASHHHAAAA!" Yasmine yelled.

"SASHA COME DOWNSTAIRS!" Candy yelled right along with her.

"We don't even know if her window is in the front guys," I said.

"Well we about to find the fuck out now," Candy said right as the girl from Instagram appeared behind the window.

"Who the fuck are y'all?" she yelled.

"If you know Trey then you know who the fuck I am!" I yelled suddenly getting a voice out of nowhere.

"Oh, was sup Emerald," she had the audacity to say.

"Bitch come downstairs! You had all that energy playing on my phone!" I yelled.

"Yeah bitch to leave my man alone! We are starting a family and don't have time for this. He said you delusional and won't leave him alone so that's why I stepped in between," She said.

Delusional? Family? What?

"Bitch Trey don't even want kids!" I yelled.

"Well that's not what he told me!" She yelled as she rubbed her belly. It felt like the whole world just stopped moving. She's pregnant? What?

"Bitch I don't give a fuck! Your face isn't pregnant!" Candy yelled.

I was so embarrassed at this point I had to get out of here so I told them that we should just leave. Me and Candy got in the car first. I knew they felt bad for me from the looks on their faces.

"Scary hoe!" Yasmine yelled and got in the car. How did my life turn into this? How could he do this to me? He's really having a baby after he made me get rid of mines.

Almost one year ago...

Tonight, was the night. The night I was going to tell Trey I was pregnant. I knew he was going to be excited because this is what he said he wanted. I've been feeling nauseous for a while, but I didn't pay it any mind. I took a test and it was negative, so I figured it was just my mind playing tricks of me. But when I missed my period? I knew it was something more to it. Going to the doctor, they just confirmed what I already knew. Tonight, I cooked for Trey and I was going to tell him over dinner. After eating we were lying in bed and I told him I had a surprise for him.

"Baby, I know you been wanting this for a while now. You're going to be dad!" I yelled to him while holding up a positive test. The look on his face I couldn't really read so I was a little confused.

"Your pregnant?" He asked.

"Yes," I replied

"I thought you was on birth control?"

"I stopped taking it after you told me you wanted a baby."

"Oh," he responded.

Sitting on the bed I felt my vision getting blurry. This was not the response I thought I was going to get.

"This is not what you wanted?" I asked him.

"Yes and no. Just not right now with all this stuff I got going on," he had the nerve to say.

"So why would you tell me you wanted a baby?" I cried.

I never gotten pregnant before but the thought of getting rid of the baby killed me. I didn't want to raise my baby alone. How can he do this to me?

"At that time, I did," he said

"Trey that was only a month ago!"

"A lot of shit can happen in a month!" He yelled back at me.

"Look baby I'm sorry, it just happened so soon. I'm just not ready for one right now. When shit settle down then I can give you all the babies in the world okay," he said then kissed me on the forehead.

I cried myself to sleep that night knowing god was going to punish me for what I was going to do.

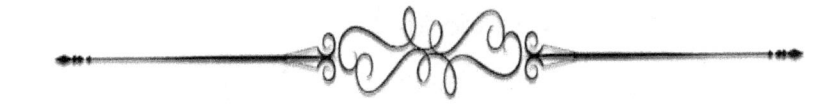

Present...

Three hours later we were all drunk at Nas house. I was so glad to have my girls here with me. I called Trey and he didn't even answer none of my calls. I know he knew what happened and was dodging me. Candy was mad at Nas thinking he knew, and Yasmine was sad over Yasir still. We was all fucked up right now. I went to the bathroom and looked in the mirror. Was it something wrong with me? Was that the reason why he did this to me? Yasmine was passed out in the guest room and Candy went to bed with Nas. I was up all alone, and I couldn't sleep. I heard noise from the basement and went downstairs to see who was down there. I saw Vito down there rolling a blunt. He had his dreads up in a bun and some black sweats on.

"Hey."

"Was sup," he replied nonchalantly.

"So, you just going to not respond to my messages?" I asked him.

"What you wanted? Somebody to talk to you while your MIA. I'm not the one for that."

"I thought we were friends!"

"Yeah I can't be friends with you. Sorry Emerald."

"Why not? Why Vito?" I asked. Yes, my feelings was hurt.

"Because I like you and I respect your relationship enough to walk away," he said. *Ha! What relationship?*

"I'm not in a relationship."

He started laughing.

"Okay Emerald."

I got on the bed next to him and sat down.

"Vito I'm serious it's over," I told him.

"Oh, that's why you came down here to talk to me. What you trying to get revenge or something?" He asked.

"No, I just miss my friend that's all."

"Hmm okay."

"Can I hit that?" I asked.

"Emerald you don't smoke," he said as he lit his blunt.

"Yeah well it's a first time for everything right? You know a lot about first times," I said, and he laughed.

He showed me how to smoke it and I took a puff. I immediately felt the effects of the weed.

"Does it always make you feel like this?" I asked.

"Not all. I just got some good shit that's why," he said.

I nodded and took another pull. With also the effects of the liquor we had earlier I was feeling it even more.

"Aight that's enough. Before your ass start going crazy."

He took the blunt and finished smoking as he played the game. His brown strong arms was flexing as he controlled the joystick. He was so damn fine I regretted letting him go while I was being cheated on anyway so technically, I didn't start the cheating. I got closer to him.

"What?" He asked.

"Where my hug at?" I asked boldly.

He paused the game and faced me and gave me a hug. He was trying to let me go but I grabbed him tighter.

"I missed you," I whispered in his ear.

"Oh really?" He asked.

"Yes. I miss my friend," I told him.

I let him go and got on top of him.

"Emerald what are you doing?"

"I'm going to show you how much I miss you."

I came closer to him and started kissing him. I felt his dick growing under me, so I knew he liked what I was doing.

"Vito fuck me please," I begged and started grinding on his dick.

"No Em. Not like this this. I can't," he said.

"Why not?" I asked.

"Because I don't want you to regret it."

And on that note, he moved me from off him and finished playing his game. I watched him play the game until I fell asleep.

Yasmine

    Today was the day I was going to get my man back. You cannot just come into my life and make orders and then disappear. No, it don't work like that. Yeah, I made a tiny little mistake, but he cannot knock me for doing something I am used to and that was paying my bills. During one of our conversation he stated he need help at the store and that can be a way for us to spend more time with one another while I still work, but I just wanted to find something on my own. Walking into his store I saw the same lady from when I came in here the first time. I never came in again, but I saw that she remembered my face. Technically that's my man so I didn't have to ask to go to his office.

    Knock! Knock!

    "Miss you cannot go back there," she told me.

    Ignoring her I knocked again.

Yasir came to the door and opened it. Walking inside I closed the door and walked right to his desk. It had paperwork everywhere. Maybe he did need some help.

"I'm busy right now Yasmine," he told me.

"Me too," I replied.

He sat back down and put his head back into his work.

"SOOO, I was thinking that we should just move past this," I told him.

"Okay," he laughed sarcastically.

Okay that didn't work, I thought.

Walking towards him I came and sat on the desk.

"Yasir I'm really sorry, you're not even being open minded and seeing it from my perspective," I told him.

Sitting back in his chair, he gave me his full attention.

"I'm listening," he said.

"Uh-" was the only thing that came out of my mouth.

Okay, granted. I did come here to plead my case, but he was looking to fine now. Leaning back in his chair his dick print was visible though his slacks. His black button up shirt looked as if it was custom fitted just for him. I cannot believe I never noticed how fine he was.

"Okay so like I was saying, you just came and told me to stop working. I'm an independent woman and don't depend on only myself. How was I going to make my money? Who was going to take care of me— "

"I gave you an offer," he projected.

"Yes, Yasir I know."

"What you think I'm going to under pay you?" he asked.

"No, I never stated that, I just... what if it goes bad between us, then what?" I asked him.

"Why would it go bad between us?"

"Something's just happen Yasir!" I yelled.

"Yeah. When you think negative you speak it into existence," he replied

Yes, indeed he was right.

"Maybe I was wrong, and I can admit that. I'm just a man that doesn't like to waste time and if I claim you as my woman, then that's what it's going to be. Yeah this could've been your first and last time doing that shit behind my back but who's to know you won't do anything else behind my back? Being sneaky is how trust issues get involved," he said.

"Yessss baby I know and I'm sorryyy," I told him.

"Well I still need some time," he said.

"Fuck time!" I said as we both laughed.

I went to him and sat on his lap with us positioned face to face.

"Well I missed you just a little something, something," He said.

"Oh, word it's like that?" I asked, acting hurt.

"Nah you know I missed you sexy," he said grabbing my head and kissing me.

Grrrrrr, my stomach growled.

"Oops," I laughed

"Damn baby you hungry?" He asked me.

"Yes, I was too nervous to eat before I came," I said.

"It's cool, we can go to one of these restaurants in the mall or close by," he said.

"Okay" I smiled.

I told him I always wanted to try this new place I heard of called "Vervain" so that's where we decided to go. It wasn't in the mall, but it was close by. He decided to go with the Lobster tail, Cajun shrimp and a side of mash with asparagus. I went along and got what he ordered because it sounded good. We started to talk about his daughter, and I loved the look he would get in his eyes whenever we would talk about her. Maybe it's because my father wasn't present in my life, but I respected Yasir for being a dad. A great one at that.

"So, what happened with you and her mom?" I asked him.

"She was young and didn't want to settle down. Took advantage of me but she's nothing you must worry about. We weren't together in years," He assured me.

"Oh, okay that's cool," I responded.

"Hey Bambi," I heard someone say.

I turned around and was surprised to see Cinnamon.

"Hey," I quickly responded.

Why she was talking to me like we were cool or something?

"I don't see you around at the club anymore," she said.

"Yeah because I don't work there anymore," I answered.

"Oh, you too good now?" She pressed.

"Girl get out of my face," I responded putting my attention back on Yasir.

"Baby you ready?" I heard a familiar voice say.

I turned back around and was surprised to see it was Jay.

"Yes, I'm ready," I heard Cinnamon say proudly.

I busted out laughing because this had to be a joke.

"Something funny bitch? You mad I took your man?" Cinnamon asked.

"Girl no! That's all you," I responded. Now I see why she broke her neck to say hi.

"Baby she isn't nothing but a hoe don't sweat her," Jay said.

"A hoe?! Nigga please!" I laughed.

I saw Yasir about to get up, so I grabbed his hand and told him to relax

"Yeah a fucking hoe. All I had to do was spend a little money and those legs flew open! Bitch you wasn't shit but reliable pussy," he had the nerve to say.

Me? The bitch he was crying down every day and telling he love. Me? This man obviously done went mad.

"Nigga don't get mad you was just a trick, please." I said.

That must have ticked him off because his bitch ass grabbed me by my hair.

"Stupid bitch that's why your father don't love your hoe ass—" I was so in shocked and was confused to why I didn't hear him talking anymore. The father line was a low blow. One day I was in my feelings and I slipped up and told him about me and my father relationship. I looked up and he was knocked out on the floor. Yasir spit on him and kicked him, he seemed more upset than me.

"Nigga talk so much and all it took was one fucking hit?!" Yasir yelled.

I was so embarrassed because so many people were watching us. Yasir grabbed somebody phone who was recording and broke it with his bare two hands.

"Come on Yasir lets go," I said and grabbed his hand.

Cinnamon was just there screaming trying to get Jay to wake up. Yasir was furious. We got in the car and he was zooming through traffic.

"Yasir calm down! You're going to get us killed!" I yelled at him.

"Who the fuck was that?! And why the fuck he was acting like that?!" He yelled

"Baby it's a long story," I responded.

"You fuck with clown ass niggas like him?"

"No, I met him at the club we were dating for a while and he's mad because I cut him off. It's nothing serious!" I yelled back.

"Give me all the information you know about him!" He yelled.

"Why?"

"Because I fucking said so that's the fuck why!" He responded

Come to think about it, I didn't really know shit about Jay. I told Yasir the most I knew just to get him to relax.

Nas

I was waiting for Candy to come to the club and bring me some food. I was so busy I didn't have no time to get any lunch.

"One of your little worker bitches was about to get it."

She came in obviously upset.

"What happened babe?" I asked her.

"The bitch talking about who I am, and I can't come up here. The bitch know who I am because obviously everybody knows! I'm not the one!" She screamed.

"Baby maybe she didn't notice you. Don't let her get you all upset," I told her.

"Yeah okay. Well she better not make any more mistakes because I will fire her ass!" She yelled.

"Baby how you trying to fire one of my employees?" I laughed. Candy ass was a mess. She started laughing too.

"Now come over here and feed your man I'm hungry," I told her. Whenever we were together, she always fed me, or I would feed her. It made the food taste so much better and over time we just got used to it. Sitting on top of my desk I got between her legs as she made a plate of food for me. I told her to get me some food from a seafood spot that was close by. She got me some steamed salmon with some shrimps and vegetables. She got a fork and started feeding me and feeding herself too. I told her to get a large because she always don't get her any food and wind up eating my shit anyway.

"So how long are we going to be in California again?" She asked me.

She thought we was just going out there to see the club but like I said before she was going to get the surprise of her life.

"Probably just a week why was sup?" I asked her.

"I think Emerald should come. She's been sad with the Trey situation that you swore up and down you didn't know about and now with your cousin. How he just leave and not even say bye?" She asked.

"I told you I didn't know shit about no baby! Me and that man don't even speak much babe. I'm not getting involved in his business. As for Vito, that's a grown ass man. Emerald knew what was up and if sis want to come to try and get Vito she could come," I laughed. *Woman*. Her ass had all the opportunities to get his ass when he was here but was playing all these games to now flying across states to get him. She thought her ass was slick.

"Well I wouldn't say that," Candy laughed.

"Yeah okay," I told her.

"I can't wait to see you all big and round. What if you have twins?" I asked her.

She always got weird when I talked about kids. I don't know if it's because she had a miscarriage before but I'm almost positive that we soon was going to have a baby. It could be something wrong with me, you never know. She didn't even respond she just went into her phone and started texting away.

"Did you hear what I said?" I asked her.

"Yes, I heard what you said," she replied with an attitude

"Whatever Candy," I said. I didn't have time to deal with her bipolar shit right now.

After Candy was done feeding me and herself, she got up to get ready to go to the salon.

"Boss man, somebody is here to see you."

Synthia came in and opened the door without even knocking. The way Candy face was looking, if you can kill somebody with looks, Synthia would've been on the floor dead.

"Bitch don't you see he's fucking busy and don't you know how to fucking knock!" Candy yelled.

"Well I was just doing my job!" Synthia yelled back.

"His name is fucking Nasir not no fucking boss man! Let me get the fuck out of here before I kill a bitch. Love you DADDY!" Candy dramatic ass kissed me like we was never going to see each other again. And walked out my office making sure to bump Synthia on the way out. This girl is crazy!

Synthia

I hated that bitch. She thought she was the shit but she's going to see. When I take her fucking man right from her! She didn't deserve somebody like Nas. He needed a real woman like me. I was a very petite woman. Standing at 5'4, I didn't have much height to me either. I was mixed with Colombian and Italian. My hair was long to my ass and I always kept it bone straight. I was small but I had some big titties I always wore out just for Nasir. I know that bitch was just using him for his money. I can spot a gold-digging hoe from a mile away. She better had been glad I needed this job because I would've snatched that long ass ponytail right off her head. She think she got the upper hand now but that bitch soon will see.

"Why did you act like you didn't know who she was?" Toya asked. She was one of the workers here too.

"I didn't know it was her," I shrugged.

Yeah, I did know but so the fuck what. Bitch coming up in here like she own the place. Bitch don't own shit!

"Synthia can you come to my office please," I heard Nas say over the speaker phone. Everybody was giving me the death glare like I was in trouble or something. I loved the way he say's my name. I walked into his office and he told me to have a seat.

"Sorry about Candy she can be a little off the wall at times." he said to me.

"It's okay boss man I understand," I said.

"And if she's around tried not to call me that to diffuse any problems for the future," he told me.

"So, what would you like for me to call you?" I asked.

"Nas is fine," He said.

"Okay Boss man Nas," I said flirting.

Yeah, I was flirting. So, what. He just started laughing and shaking his head.

"What's funny?" I asked.

"Nothing you can get back to work now," he said.

Before leaving out I purposely dropped some papers off his desk.

"Oh, sorry let me get that," I told him as I bent all the way over and picked up his papers. I turned around and he was staring at me. I knew he wanted to watch my ass.

"It's okay Synthia I got it. Get back to work!" He yelled as I scurried out of there. He won't be saying that for too long. Something told me not to wear any panties today under my skirt and I'm glad I listened to my instincts because when I bent down, I know Nas saw my pretty pussy. I needed to come up with a plan fast because I'm getting tired of waiting on what's supposed to be mine.

Yasmine

YASIR: *I wish I was with you right now.*

ME: *Yes, me too, I have things to do in the morning though.*

YASIR: *Yes, I know. It would be selfish of me, but I can't help it that I'm selfish and want you all to myself.*

ME: *Don't make me blush.*

Beep! Beep! Beep.

I looked out my window and noticed that was my car alarm going off. That was weird. I didn't think too much of it because it's always something wrong with technology. I went outside to go check on my car to make sure everything was fine with it. I've been dreading getting a new car, but it was like something new was wrong with it every day.

Walking back to my door I started to feel weird. Looking around I didn't see anyone. I walked inside and made sure I locked both locks. You know that feeling you just get out the blue? It was sort of like my gut was telling me something. I closed the blinds and turned on the TV hoping it will help me fall asleep because I was starting to feel paranoid.

An hour later...

I still couldn't sleep. I had a feeling I just couldn't shake. I texted Yasir but fifteen minutes later I still didn't receive a text back. So, I decided to call him.

"What you are doing?" I asked him as soon as he answered.

"Nothing chilling," he answered and then told me to hold on.

"Nigga I'm not cheating! Give me all my fucking money!" I heard him yell in the background.

"Yeah babe was sup? I'm just chilling playing dice," He told me.

"I'm lonely," I sadly sad.

"Lonely? What happened, you miss your man?"

"Yes, can you come get me?" I asked him.

"Come get you? Didn't you tell me you got something to do in the morning?" He asked.

"Okay forget it. Good night," I said about to hang up the phone.

"Hang up this phone. I dare you."

Silence

"Yeah that's what I thought. You shouldn't have been playing hard to get earlier but give me twenty minutes baby. You not too far from me," he replied

That was music to my ears because I started to feel like I was being watched or something. I took a shower and threw on some sweats while I waited for Yasir to arrive.

HONK!

I heard Yasir honk his horn to tell me he arrived. He could've just called me to come down but whatever it took to not be alone tonight, I was not complaining. I got in his car and put my bag in the back with some extra clothes and toiletries.

"I didn't say you could move in!" He yelled as he started driving the car.

I rolled my eyes at him because he played too damn much.

"Nah I'm just playing baby," he said.

"I have to get up early because I have an interview," I told him as he rolled his eyes.

"What now?" I asked him.

"You know how I feel about that," he said.

"Yasir I don't want this just handed to me. I told you how I felt about that," I replied.

Ever since I stopped working at the club, he offered me to come and work in his jewelry shop. I denied the offer though because I didn't want it to seem like this opportunity was just handed to me. Everything that I do I worked hard for. Maybe it was a pride thing.

"Aight Yasmine whatever you say," he replied, and we just left it at that.

I would think about the opportunity but as of right I know I will go on the job interview tomorrow.

I loved being at his home. Mainly because it was just so damn beautiful and spacious. The thing I loved the most was that his dining room ceiling was made completely out of glass. When it would start lightning, I use to be scared that the ceiling would come crashing down on us, but he reassured me that it wouldn't because of the material it was made from it. Once he did that, I felt more relaxed and admired the beauty of the lighting. Before we arrived, we went to grab some food from an Asian take out we both enjoyed. I took a quick shower and threw on one of his shirts that fitted me more like a short nightgown. Sitting at the table we started to eat our meal.

"So, you still didn't reply to your father?" He asked me.

My father or whatever you want to call him reached out to me on Facebook telling me to call him and he wanted to talk. I wanted to talk for the last twenty-eight years of my life. Yes, he was present but barely. I didn't see him in so many years and if I didn't know his name I probably wouldn't of even knew it was him.

"Nope, I don't understand why he wants to talk now," I replied.

"Well you won't know until you call him," he said

It was easy for him to say. He grew up with both parents in his household.

"I'll think about it," I replied.

I didn't like to talk about my father but I'm glad Yasir cared enough to ask about him. That's why I always had a mentality that men wasn't shit but slowly Yasir was showing me that I shouldn't just categorize all men. I expressed to him that was a soft spot for me and I'm glad he understood that. Getting up I threw our food away because we were done eating. Coming out the kitchen Yasir called me over to him. He grabbed me and sat me down on his glass table. It made me shiver from the glass being so cold.

"The table is cold," I told him trying to get up.

He still was sitting on the chair. He grabbed my legs and position my feet on his legs. Opening my legs, he licked his lips.

"What you about to do?" I asked him.

"Eat my desert," he said grabbing a fork as I started to laugh. But I can see he wasn't joking about anything. He position his chair closer to the table so that he was directly face to face with my pussy.

"You know I use to always fantasize about this moment?" He asked.

Was he talking to me or my pussy? I thought.

He came closer and kissed both of my thighs. As I looked up, I saw that it was now raining. I can hear the raindrops hitting the glass ceiling. I felt his tongue licking my clit. He was licking very slowly like he was trying to enjoy and remember every second of how I tasted. Suddenly he stopped.

"You like how that feel?" He asked me, looking up. I shook my head yes and grabbed his head to put it back where it came from. I didn't need any interruptions. This time he wasn't going slowly anymore. He put one of his fingers in my pussy while putting another one in my ass. I started grinding on fingers.

"Wait, Yasir I'm going to mess up the table," I moaned.

"Fuck the table I'll buy a new one."

He latched on my clit and started to suck it and move his fingers faster.

"I'm about to come," I moaned with my eyes shut.

Just as I was Cumming, he pushed his dick inside of me at the same thing. I was not prepared for this. I couldn't control myself; it was feeling too good. I couldn't stop screaming. He had my legs on his shoulders pounding inside of me as I laid flat on the table. He lifted me up and put my back against the wall as he kissed me with so much passion, I automatically started to come again. He was so big and strong and so gentle it made him even sexier. All I saw was us in the clouds saying I do with ten kids running around, because I was never letting this dick go. He had me hallucinating so I knew this was some dangerous dick. Somehow, someway we ended up on the floor spent and drained.

"You know you're so beautiful," he said to me playing in my hair.

I was smiling so hard as I blushed.

I can get use to this.

I woke up at one in the afternoon and Yasir was nowhere to be found. He knew I had an interview in the morning and his ass didn't even wake me before he left. How inconsiderate was that! I went to the bathroom to get myself together before I call him to curse his ass out. I grabbed a disposable toothbrush and brushed my teeth. After rinsing my mouth out, I Face timed him.

"Why didn't you wake me up?!" I yelled at him.

"Good afternoon beautiful," he smiled at me looking as handsome as ever.

"Yasir I don't appreciate how you... ahhhhhhhhhh," I suddenly screamed.

Looking into the Face Time camera I saw the diamond choker on my neck that I was mesmerized by at his jewelry store.

"No, you didn't!" I yelled.

I ran back to the bathroom admiring it. I was so pissed at him I didn't even notice.

"Well I'm still mad!" I said.

"Yeah okay. I'm not going to be at the store for long so make sure you're right where you're at now waiting on me," he said as he hung up.

Trey

 Emerald was in her feelings about finding out about Sasha. I still denied the shit because it wasn't any of her fucking business. Should've never been snooping around with her nosey ass friends! Those bitches need a fucking life. Messing my shit up! Sasha ass too! When I found out what she did I came to fuck her ass up. Pregnant or not she knew what the fuck she was doing but she put that pregnant pussy on me, and I forgot about everything. What they say about pregnant pussy is the fucking truth for real. Emerald ass was making me go fucking crazy because this time she seemed serious about leaving my ass alone. She can't fucking leave me until I tell her ass too. What the fuck she think this shit is? I'm not done with her ass. She better not be giving up my fucking pussy either or I'm going hurt her ass. I'm trying to be patient with her, but she is really testing me.

"The number you reached is not in service."

Oh, hell no! I know her ass didn't change her fucking number on me. That bitch is really feeling herself! She know she's nothing without me. I pulled up to her apartment because she moved all her shit out of my place. I got out the car and banged up on her door.

"EMERALD! BRING YOUR STUPID ASS DOWNSTAIRS!" I yelled.

I was ringing the shit out of her bell.

"Trey go away before I call the cops."

"You stupid bitch if you got somebody up there, I'm going to kill you and him!"

Walking to the car I got here that I knew she loves so much, I went in my pocket, grabbed my knife and popped a hole in in. I did it with so much force, I wasn't expecting to hear it pop. It made me feel a little good to get my anger out. I knew she loved this car so much and I brought it with my own money so I could do whatever it was I wanted to do with it. Going to each tire, one by one, I popped each tire. Kicking it, punching the windows, I was trying my best to destroy this car.

"Trey my fucking car! Are you serious?! You know I have to work!" she cried.

"Take a taxi bitch!" I yelled and got in my car.

I knew somebody called the cops already, so I had to get missing.

"What Sasha?" I answered the phone.

"Trey I'm on my way to the hospital I'm in laborrrr. It's too soon. I'm scared and it hurts," she cried.

If it wasn't one thing it was something fucking else. She told me what hospital she was going to, and I stayed on the phone with her the whole time. Emerald ass was lucky because I was just going to park around the corner so I can see if she got a Nigga coming out of her crib. I'm going to catch up with her ass soon!

Emerald

This man obviously lost his fucking marbles. My fucking car?! Is he serious? I can't believe he would do this. He's the one that got caught fucking cheating, not me.

"What am I going to do?" I cried into the phone with Candy. He was scaring me now. I knew he had a little anger issues, but this is off the wall. I was scared he might hurt me.

"You can come with me and Nas to California for the weekend. You need to get away from there because he's going insane," She suggested.

"California? I can't go there I'm not prepared," I told her. She should've told me this ahead of time.

"It's okay girl we just going to see the club they have down there. Just pack a few things I'm going to book you a ticket for flying now. Nas got some hotel connects so I know you can get a room for free. Pleaseeeee," she begged.

"Okay. When are you guys leaving?" I asked.

"Tomorrow."

"Tomorrow?! Candy!"

"Yes, tomorrow pleaseeee Emmy," she begged.

"Okay. A little hot weather won't kill me," I laughed.

"YES! Just take it as a birthday present," She said.

Birthday? Shit with all this shit that's going on I forgot about my own damn birthday, I thought.

"Well I'm getting ready to come to the salon so Simone can hook me up really quick."

"I'm having Nas come and get you I don't trust that bum," she said

"Candy no, I can take a cab or something," I told her.

"Yeah the fuck right not on my watch. I'm calling him now."

She hung up on me and I started getting ready because I knew Nas would be here any second now.

The plane was finally landing, and I couldn't wait to get off. I needed to get away from New York and Trey crazy ass! I can't believe he had the audacity to do that to my car.

"So tonight, we are going to go to the BLACKOUT they have out here. This was the first one ever and I'm excited to go," Candy said

"So that means Vito is going to be there?" I asked.

"Maybe, he knows we came out here so it's possible," Candy said.

That means I was going to have to look real cute tonight. I was done playing games with him. I hope it's not too late though. I missed his ass like hell. I missed our talks even more. I felt such like a fool letting a good man slip right through my fingers over Trey dog ass. I bought a nice cute green bodysuit too. It wasn't going to be no way that he can deny me!

After taking a nap and getting situated in my hotel room I started to get dress. Candy said she and Nas would be here around ten and it was nine-thirty now, so I was right on time. I took a few selfies and posted it on my Instagram. Of course, without my location. The way Trey was moving. I was not taking any chances with him. Candy messaged me and told me to come downstairs. I saw them right in the front, so I walked to the car.

"You're going to get your man back girl," she said laughing.

Nas just shook his head and turned up the music.

Like the other BLACKOUTS it was dark inside but instead of the glass with the fish inside it just had mirrors everywhere. I guess they came up with the fish idea after this one was made. This was still as nice though. We walked into a section and I saw Vito drinking from a bottle of ace of spades like he normally do. I was going to walk over to him, but when I saw a girl come to him and sit on his lap. *Excuse me?* Candy must have saw the look on my face because she grabbed me, and we walked towards the bar.

"Did you fucking see that?"

"Yes. I don't think he knew you was coming Emerald I don't know," she said.

"I'm about to go," I said.

"No, you're not. We are going to enjoy ourselves. You left New York for a reason. If that's what he want, then fuck him!" She yelled.

She was right. I'm tired of stressing myself over these niggas.

"Let me get a double shot of patron," I told the bartender. After I took the shots, we made our way back the section. The girl was dancing on Vito all crazy. She wasn't even as cute as me! The nerve of him. I guess he was surprised to see me because he was just staring at me.

After an hour of drinking and partying I was feeling myself. I gave a few people my number and forgot all about Vito. I came out here to enjoy myself, not to be stressed over the next man.

Candace

"Baby I'm going to go find Emerald," I told Nas as I kissed him and saw Vito roll his eyes. Obviously, somebody was in their feelings. Walking to the bar I saw Emerald having a conversation with a guy. She was obviously more on the drunk side because if she was sober, she would've seen this man was ugly as hell.

"Hey Candy! This is my new friend John. John this is my best friend Candy," she said.

"Nice to meet you John. Emerald let's go," I said as I grabbed her. We went to the other side of the bar and I ordered me a margarita. As I grabbed my margarita, I heard somebody tell me excuse me. I turned around and got the fucking surprise of my life. I dropped my whole drink and the glass splattered everywhere.

"Deuce?!" I yelled.

It was him, it had to be him.

Emerald was looking just a shock as me. She knew all about Deuce.

"Candy?" He asked. He was just as fine as the first day I laid eyes on him. A little bigger of course from him being in jail. He was the only Italian guy I ever dealt with. Last time I saw him he had a head full of long beautiful hair. Now, it was cut off into a curly Fro. His beautiful hazel eyes was looking at me with sorrow. All type of emotions came crashing down one by one and suddenly I started to feel angry.

"You left me without any explanation! Cut off all contact and all! I hate you!" I slapped him and screamed as tears came crashing down my face. I ran to the bathroom with Emerald hot on my tail.

"Oh noooo," she slurred while she shook her head pacing back and forth. She looked like she was the one going through this and not me.

"Candy girl you going to have to wipe your face and act like this never happened before Nas see's you," she said to me. Shit for a little minute I forgot all about Nas and where I was at.

Shit!

We stayed in the bathroom for about ten minutes and finally left.

"I can't stay in here while Deuce is here. I have to go," I told Emerald.

"I understand Candy," she said as we approached the section.

"What happened baby? You okay?" Nas asked me.

"Yeah babe we had a little girl talk that's all," I said laughing.

He looked a little suspicious but let it go. Thank god!

Vito

Why the fuck was Emerald out here? Nas didn't tell me she was coming. Chantel left and I was glad because the death stares Emerald was giving me was getting on my nerves. Well now she see what happens when you want to play games.

"Vito you mind taking Emerald back to the hotel since you go that way?" Nas had the nerve to ask me.

Me and her didn't say one word to each other. Hell, no I didn't want to take her, but I wasn't going to be a bitch about it.

"Yeah I'll take her," I told him.

We all got ready to go and Emerald said her goodbyes to Nas to and Candy.

"You don't have to walk so fast!" She said trying to catch up with me.

Shit the faster I walk the faster I can get her back to the hotel.

"So, catch up," I told her.

I heard her suck her teeth.

Finally getting too into my Black Beemer she got in and slammed the door.

"Watch the fucking door!" I told her.

"Why you being so mean to me? Who was that your girlfriend?" She asked question after another.

"Don't worry about who that was. Worry about your man,"

"Bitch," I heard her mumble.

"What you said?"

"Nothing, nothing at all."

She started texting away on her phone. Probably texting Candy talking about me as if I gave a fuck.

We finally reached the hotel and it's been almost two minutes and she didn't get out of the car yet.

"Can you walk me upstairs? I'm scared," she said.

"Scared? Scared of what?" I asked her.

"I don't want to talk about it now I'm just asking for a favor," she had the nerve to have an attitude.

I parked the car and got out while she walked ahead of me. She had on a green body suit that showed all her curves and some gold heels and a gold clutch. If I wasn't mad at her I would've given her a compliment, but she didn't need to hear that from me.

We finally got to the elevator and she pressed the 18th floor.

"Did you ever stay at this hotel before?" She asked me.

"Yeah."

"Oh okay."

Walking towards her door she stopped in front of it and thanked me.

"You can come in for a little if you want," she said.

"No, it's okay I'm aight. It was nice seeing you."

I tried to walk away but she pulled me back and into the room.

"You don't miss me?" she asked.

"No."

I was lying but she didn't need to know that.

"Oh, okay well I miss you," she said.

She walked towards the bed in the hotel and started to take off her body suit that she was completely naked underneath.

"What are you doing?" I asked her.

"I want to show you something," she said.

She grabbed one of the chairs and put it directly in front of the bed. I knew she was a little drunk, so I was a little suspicious to what the hell she was up to. Grabbing my hand, she told me to sit in the chair and I did. Walking to the radio she hooked her phone up and put on some R&B music.

Sitting directly in front of me on the bed she laid back and opened her legs giving me a full view of her pussy.

"You can look but you can't touch," she said.

She started to rub on her pussy and her nipples. Damn she was a freak. I don't know if the liquor helped and gave her the courage, but she was turning me the fuck on. She started to fuck her pussy with her fingers, and she was so wet you can hear it. My dick started growing in my pants. The room light wasn't on but from the streetlights outside I could see her perfectly.

"Hmmm Vitooo," she moaned.

I went closer and started to kiss on her inner thigh as she started going faster and faster.

"No, you can't touch," she said and moved my head away.

She was enjoying the hell out of this. My dick felt like it was going to bust through my jeans. She turned around and was on all fours on the bed now still playing with her pussy. I couldn't control it anymore. I got closer and bit her ass.

"Vito, I said no touching!"

"Shut the fuck up! You can't have no pussy in my face telling me don't touch you!" I told her.

I started to take my clothes off and pulled my dick out and put it in her pussy.

"Wait Vito be gentle."

"Don't you want this dick? You been trying to give me this pussy for a minute. I don't want to hear that crying shit."

Fuck, her ass looked so sexy. My dick was covered in her wetness as I moved in and out of her. Damn I think this was the best pussy I ever had. I knew her ass was going to have some fucking good pussy. I turned her down one time, but I wasn't doing that again. You wanted to give me some pussy? I was going to take it. I guess hitting from the back was too much for her right now. Ima let her slide because it's the first time, but she better get used to it. I told her to get on top of me. Right when she got on top of me just on cue, I hear the song Anywhere by 112 in the background.

I love the way your body feels
On top of mine so take your time
We got a night
Girl, you know
I like it slow
And I know you like it too, baby
Please don't stop I feel it now
You feel it, too

You're shivering
Ooh, you put me close to you
Just let it flow
There's no other place to go

I guess Emerald was listening to the song too because she was moving to the beat. I grabbed her ass with my left hand and started grinding under her. It was like her pussy fit my dick perfectly.

"Vito baby yes I needed this dick," She moaned riding the shit out of my dick as she came. She wasn't going slow or complaining about the size anymore. Shit was feeling too good I kept telling her to slow down but her ass wouldn't listen. I turned her around and was on top now. She was making some sexy love faces. I bent down and kissed her.

"You know that's the first time you came on my dick?" I asked her. She just shook her head up and down.

"You want to come on this dick again?"

She shook her head up and down again.

"I can't hear you."

"Yes baby! Yes!" She moaned.

I started pumping in and out of her faster and faster while playing with her pussy. After a few strokes I felt so much wetness squirting out of her pussy.

"Wait Vito what happened?" She asked looking shocked.

"That pussy talking to me baby," I told her going slower now.

"Oh my god that never happened to me before," she said.

"It's okay baby. You know I'm the man of first times," I told her.

Her pussy felt so damn good I didn't want to get out of it. She told me she couldn't take it anymore, so I finally released. After wiping me and her down I got in the bed with her.

"Emerald," I called her name out

"Hmmm?" she answered half sleep.

"Happy birthday baby."

I kissed her and closed my eyes. A nigga was drained.

Synthia

This bitch Candy was always posting shit about Nas all over Instagram. I hated that shit. He was supposed to be with me! Before he opened the club, I stayed and put in hours making sure it was going to be perfect just to satisfy him. Imagine my fucking surprise when I saw Candy coming over to the club a lot. Nas was so perfect. The perfect gentleman. He treated all of us with respect and cared about all our person needs. I loved coming into work just to see him. Sometimes I would make mistakes with my work just so he can call me up to his office. Each time he would call me I would make sure to drop hints that I wanted his ass. He was supposed to be my man! Not hers! I even knew him longer than she did! What was it that she had that I didn't have?

One thing I knew she had was that salon! Which I was on my way to now. She wanted to be a showoff and post all their business on Instagram, so I knew they were currently in California. I pulled up to the salon and went towards the back door. I threw a brick in her office window. Oh, this bitch must have really thought she was untouchable. I destroyed her office from the papers to cutting up her leather couches. I destroyed it all!!! Satisfied with my work I made my way to the floor of the salon. I grabbed all the acetone and poured it all over the floor. I grabbed the acrylic powder and acetone and put it all over the stations. Ha! They would need to buy some new tools. Grabbing the bleach, I made even more of a mess. I broke all the mirrors in the salon and ruined all the chairs. I even made a mess in the bathroom with some shit I got off the street from a dog and squashed it all over the mirror and toilet. Looking at all my work I smiled on the inside. Candy wouldn't be at the club a lot anymore! She's going to be too busy trying to bring her salon back to life again. So, I can have Nas all to myself without that hoe in the way!

Nas

Today was going to be the big day. The day I was going to ask Candy to be my wife. Wasn't any doubt in my mind that she wouldn't say yes. I know we haven't been together for years, but I knew and felt in my heart this was it. I just couldn't believe I will soon be a married man. The thought of being married never crossed my mind until Candy appeared. She wanted to go to the mall to get a few things. After going to damn near every store in the mall. I had to make about three damn trips to the car.

"Baby I promise this is the last store," she begged.

Now I remember why I didn't like going shopping with her to begin with. I stood outside the store because I was not with the questions about how this and that look when quite frankly all the shit looked the same!

About fifteen minutes later we was finally walking to the car. She put her purse in the back seat to put the rest of the bags in the trunk and her purse fell over. All her vitamins fell everywhere. I picked them up and toss them on the ground.

"Baby? What are you doing? Don't throw them away!" She yelled.

"Candy they were on the floor of the car."

"So, what! That don't mean throw them away!"

"It's a fucking pharmacy in the damn mall! It's not that serious we can get you as many bottles as you want!"

She looked confused.

"No baby it's okay I don't have to buy it when I have some here." she said as she put some more back inside the container.

"Candy are you fucking serious?" I pressed.

"YES! I'm deadass serious!" She yelled.

I never knew vitamins was that serious. I took the little broom I had in the car and was sweeping them out the car. She came to the side of the car I was in and grabbed the broom and threw it. What the fuck is wrong with her?

"All of this over fucking vitamins candy?"

"They're not fucking vitamins Nasir!" She yelled.

"Then what the fuck are they? I questioned.

"Birth control," she mumbled.

"Excuse me what did you say they were?!!!!"

"I said its birth control."

I cannot fucking believe her. Ever since we got together, she's been taking these damn fucking vitamins or what the fuck ever them shits was.

"Candy why the fuck are you taking birth control?!!"

"Because I'm scared to get pregnant!" She screamed with tears running down her face.

"Scared of fucking what? That I might leave you or something?" I asked.

"No, I'm scared I might lose the baby Nas and you will leave me because I'm not strong enough to carry your babies." she cried even harder.

I can't believe her. All this time I'm telling her I want kids and she's telling me she's going to give me children. She been playing me behind my back taking birth control for two years. I concluded that maybe it was me and not her. All this time she was playing me like a fucking fool when we could've been adults and talked about this shit. I can't believe this was Candy. My Candy. I left her ass sitting there in the parking lot and drove off. I was just about to ask her sneaky ass to marry me. I was going back to New York fuck all this shit.

Emerald

Two weeks later

Life was good. Seems to me like Trey disappeared off the face of the earth which was great. Me and Vito was still going strong. I'm so mad I wasted so much time away from him dealing with Trey shit. He still was in California and wanted me to come back out there. I rushed me and Trey relationship and I didn't want to rush this one. I just wanted to take things very slow. Vito was everything that I imagined in a man. Sexy, thoughtful, and did I say sexy? I had to break him in a little because he didn't believe I was fully done with Trey but after a little more begging and pleading I got him right where I wanted him. California might have not been great for Nas and Candy, but I believe in them and I know they could get through this for sure.

    Vito offered to buy me a new car, but I declined. I didn't want a man to feel like everything I had was because of him. I walked to my rental drinking my water. I haven't been feeling too good these past few days. Maybe it was something that I ate who knows. I had a client to go and show a house to. The place was so far but I needed to get me a new car and didn't have time to be lazy...

    After driving for like four hours I finally got to my destination. The area was open with not so many houses around. I told the client to be here at six and it was now five thirty, so I had enough time to blow before the client got here. Walking inside the house, I tried to turn on the lights, but it wouldn't turn on. How was I going to show a client a house in the dark? I pulled my phone out to call the client to see if maybe we can reschedule or find a way to deal with this light problem. I took my phone out and walked towards the door. I was pulled back and my phone fell. I was trying to fight the person off me but was suddenly hit in the head with a sharp object and everything went black.

Nas

I missed the hell out of Candy, but I'm still pissed the fuck off. I been at the club mostly every night now and not home. I just couldn't deal with her right now and needed more time to myself. If she could lie to me about that. No telling what else she lied to me about. I was drinking more and more to get my mind off her strangling her ass.

"Yeah Candy?" I answered my phone.

"Can we please just talk so you can understand stand why—" she begged.

"Understand why what? Why you lied to me? Help me fucking understand."

"Matter fact you had a fucking long ass time to tell me why. Don't tell me why now that your sneaky ass got fucking caught!" I yelled at her and hung up.

I took my bottle of Henny and drunk from the bottle.

I woke up to my dick inside a wet mouth. I didn't know I dozed off. It was pitch black inside of my office so I couldn't see shit. I remember having the lights on before I fell asleep so how the fuck it got turned off?

"Move Candy. Don't think just because you are sucking my dick, I'm going to forgive you."

I tried to push her away, but she wouldn't move. She started sucking harder and harder. Damn this shit was feeling fucking good so fuck it. I let her finish doing what she was doing. I didn't have no sex in two damn weeks, so I needed this. It don't mean I forgave her ass though. I reached for my bottle in the darkness and took some more to the head.

She stopped sucking my dick and sat on my shit. She started moving up and down on my dick.

"Hmm Boss man I knew you had some good dick," I heard Synthia moan.

What the fuck?

Before I could even push her the fuck off. The door to my office opened and the light turned on. What I saw made me sick to my fucking stomach. Synthia on my dick and Candy standing at the door with her face in pure disgust.

Candace

As if I needed this extra shit added to my life. I come to my salon and it was barely recognizable. I can't believe somebody had the audacity to do this. I did not need this right now. With Nas still mad at me this wasn't a good time at all for this to occur. I know he was upset and disappointed in me, but he didn't even give me a chance to explain myself. I felt like that was so unfair for one.

    I missed Nas like hell and couldn't believe he was treating me like this. As time went by, I just got used to it. It's like everything was suddenly hitting me at once. With Deuce and then Nas finding out about my birth control and now my Salon! I just didn't know if I was coming or going. Deuce was my first love. We were irresistible. He was a few years older than me, but age wasn't nothing but a number when it came to us. I wanted to give him everything and more. The only thing that I couldn't give him was a fucking child. He was understanding like shit and I loved him more for that. Deuce was heavy in the drug game and whatever happened to him I was going to make sure to ride to the end with him. He made me the person that I am now. He looked out for me and motivated the shit out of me. He was my everything. One day, I suddenly got a call telling me to leave the house because the feds might come and raid it. I left, leaving everything behind. I was wondering what the fuck was going on. I didn't hear from Deuce in months. One day I got a phone call from him.

"Hello?" I answered.
"Candy. It's me Deuce."
I immediately started crying.
"Baby what happened to you? I thought you was dead. The feds raided the house I have nothing left," I cried.
"Look I left something for you. Remember that spot I told you to go to if something like this happened?" He asked.
"Yes," I answered.
"That should have you good for a few years okay baby. I don't know how long I'm going to be gone," he said.
"Gone? Baby where are you so I can come see you?" I asked him.

"No Candy! It's not safe for you to come and see me I don't want them fucking with you. Don't wait for me baby. You're young and still got your whole life ahead of you," he said.

"Deuce no. What are you talking about? I'm not living life if you're not in it baby. You know how I feel about you," I cried.

I was so confused, why was he treating me like this.

"I have to go Candy. Just know I will always love you," he said hanging up.

That's the last time I ever spoke to him. Until I saw him in California. Snapping me out of my thoughts I got a text message.

DADDY: *Come to the club now!*

You didn't have to tell me fucking twice. I didn't even respond I jumped my ass up and hopped to the club speeding like a bat out of lighting. When I got to the club I went through the back door. I walked up the stairs and towards Nas office. I thought my ears were deceiving me. It sounded like moans and grunts was coming from inside his office. Oh, hell fucking no! Then what I heard broke my heart into fucking pieces *"Hmm Boss man I knew you had some good dick."*

I opened the door and turned on the light. To my surprise I saw Synthia with the biggest smile on her face and Nas looking like a deer caught in headlights. I just turned around and ran out the club. I couldn't believe I got my heart broken again. This time I think it might have been worst.

I pulled up to my apartment calling Emerald, but her phone kept going straight to voicemail. I needed somebody to talk to bad. I called my cousin Yasmine.

"Yasmine Nas cheated on meeeee," I cried.

"He fucking what? Are you sure?!!" She yelled.

"Yes, I saw him with my own two eyes. I saw the bitch riding his dick Yasmine!" I cried.

"Wait, where are you I'm coming to get you now."

A Silver Audi pulled up with the brightest headlights I ever saw in my life. The lights were so fucking bright it damn near blinded me. The driver turned the lights off and rolled the windows down.

"Deuce?"

"Deuce?!! Candy where the fuck are you? Don't do anything dumb now!" She yelled.

Fuck what she thought! I hung up on her ass!

"You are getting in or what?" He asked.

I walked over to the car and got in the passenger seat.

Fuck Nas!

P.S Make sure you leave a review!! Being that I am a new author I would greatly appreciate it so that it can attract new readers.

I hoped you enjoyed my first Novel.

-Sabrina Rose

CPSIA information can be obtained
at www.ICGtesting.com
Printed in the USA
LVHW021536011119
636085LV00009B/334/P

9 781728 944753